My Life Journey
Challenge & Triumphs from D.C. to DR

Coach Dr. Kevin Wilbon Sr,
Ed.D., MAED, MBA, BS, AA
Coach, Author, Military Veteran, Educator & Motivational Speaker

1846 E Innovation Park Dr STE 100 Oro Valley, AZ 85755
1-855-674-2878 | info@stonehengeliterary.com

Stonehenge Literary and Media is committed to excellence in the
publishing
Industry.

Published in the United States of America

ISBN: 978-1-0880-7628-6

eBook ISBN: 978-1-0880-7630-9

Dedication

This book is dedicated to my entire family starting off with the Wilsons, Brooks, Masons, Washingtons, Whites and Andersons. It is also dedicated to all of the special people I crossed paths with in my life – those people who gave me the special wisdom and knowledge along my journey from childhood to adulthood.

Finally, I would like to affectionately dedicate this book to my mother, Phyllis Elizabeth Brooks Wilson, and father, Calvin Wilson Jr. Thank you for instilling the concept of hard work and showing how dedication and perseverance are the routes to success and anything worth having. Both of you are my Angels watching over me.

Coach Dr. Wilson's parents at their wedding Calvin Wilson & Phyllis E. Brooks Wilson

Rest in Peace,

I love you.

Dr. Kevin Wilborn Sr. With his dad and three sons

Acknowledgment

"The world is your oyster, but it's you who decides how far you are willing to swim, and how deep you are willing to go to obtain it."

Coach Dr. Kevin Wilbon Sr.

I would like to thank my dissertation Chairs, Dr. Maggie Broderick, for her time and expertise in my journey at North Central University and Dr. Michael Pielkasch for his guidance and patience during my difficult years at Argosy Univeristy prepping me for writing to get me to the next level. Thank you both for giving me the extra needed push in finally getting my Doctoral Degree in education.

I want to thank my family and friends who believed I could accomplish this goal even when I wanted to throw the towel and my confidence wavered.

To my wife, Chris, who is a college graduate from Central Texas College, and was a major driving force leading me to complete all five of my degrees and keeping me grounded in my priorities.

Dr. Kevin Wilson Sr.'s wife –Chris Artise Wilson

I would like to thank my three intelligent sons, Kevin Jr.; who is a college graduate from Virginia State University, Kevon; a two-time college graduate from Southern Maryland Community College and University of Maryland Global Campus and, last but not least, my youngest, Christian; who is attending Westlake High School in Waldorf Maryland as a freshman.

Christian Wilson: Westlake Bulldog

Coach Wilson with Christian and the Westlake Bulldogs of Waldorf Maryland

Christian Wilbon: Waldorf Wildcats

Christian Wilbon: Westlake HS Freshman Track Runner

He has a 4.28 GPA and has been recently inducted into The National Society of High School Scholars. He is also a nationally ranked track star in his own right as an eleven-time AAU National All-American, seven-time AAU Jr. Olympian Medalist with over 200 medals. He is destined to be great once he hits college.

Christian Wilson: AAU All-American Jr. Olympian Track Star

All my kids are my rock and are very instrumental in what I've done over the years. Who would've thought I would have all these college graduates in my immediate family? I'm definitely blessed.

I would like to thank my brothers and sisters, Richard and Joyce Brown Wilson, Daryl, Calvin, Sean, and Elicia Wilson, Sharon and Reggie Collins, and Becky Ule for believing in me and knowing that I could do whatever I put my mind to.

I would like to thank my sister-in-law, Cheryl Roach, and brother-in-law, Rodney Roach, for always reminding me that I need to stick to what I'm doing and finishing up the process.

I would also like to acknowledge some special people in my life – first is my aunt, Renee Brooks, for her persuasiveness in talking me into going to the next level in my educational journey. My aunt, Yvonne Gowdy, for keeping her prayers above me at all times and having faith in what I was trying to accomplish. My rock and confidant, Ma Jozerina Mason, always instilled in me that it's not how long you do the work but that you get it accomplished, and I did! I would also like to thank Reginald Mason Sr. (RIP) and Reginald Mason Jr. for the conversations we've shared over the years intellectually and about the streets of D.C.

Thanks to Tony and Shelly Rice, who always expressed their confidence in everything I've done, whether it was sports or education. I appreciate that.

I would also like to thank my friends and business partners from ABC/WBI YCF John and Tammy Wright for their trust and guidance in me, let's do this for the kids and anyone who wants to stay fit. I would also like to acknowledge my long time friend from the US Army Darrell Campbell, we've went through a lot professionally and personally and we are still friends for life. I would also like to thank my brothers in the Committed Sons Gospel Group that I had the privilege to sing with all over the DMV, Rodney Roach, Richard Pledger, Sterling Bell, Theodore Foy, and Dana Van Brakle.

Thanks to Bishop C. Anthony Mase and First Lady, Pat Lawson Mose from the Ark of Safety Church, for their spiritual guidance and blessings that kept me mentally and spiritually strong over the years leading up to this milestone. Thank everyone in my Ark family and everyone I know and who shared in my accomplishments over the years, I hope that you are proud of me.

I hope you all enjoy my story.

About the Author

Coach Dr Wilson with Thomas Stone Boys Varsity Basketball Team

Born on November 22, 1961, and raised in the urban parts of Washington D.C., Coach Dr. Kevin Wilson Sr. is one of six siblings. He is a retired US Army Military Veteran of twenty-four years, and his areas of expertise were Logistics, Arms Room Weapons NCOIC, Contracting, Transportation NCOIC, and Central Issuing Facility NCOIC, Army Drug and Alcohol Prevention and Control (ADAPC).

Currently, he also has two books available for purchase on Amazon, "Bullying and Cyberbullying in Middle Schools" and "What's your motivation?"

Coach Dr. Kevin Wilbon Sr. with his Educational Accomplishments

Coach Dr. Kevin Wilbon Sr. is an Alumni of Central Texas College of Killeen Texas, National-Louis University of Chicago Illinois, Touro University of Calamee California, and the North Central University of Scottsdale Arizona. He holds five Educational Degrees; Associates in Arts, Bachelors of Science, and Masters in Education, Masters of Business Administration (MBA), and Doctorate of Education, Educational Leadership.

Dr. Wilbon has been inducted into seven prestigious Honor Societies for his educational accomplishments. His 4.0 GPA at North Central University Honor ultimately got him inducted into these honor societies: The National Honor Society, Honor Society for Black Engineers, National Society for Collegiate Scholars, National Society of Leadership and Success, Golden Key

International Honor Society, Kappa Delta Pi Society for Educational Leaders and Strathmore's Professional Who's Who Honors and Awards.

His success doesn't end here; owning a love for achievements, Dr. Wilbon made his way to becoming a High School Varsity Basketball coach for Boys and Girls, enjoying the success in capturing three Boys Maryland State Basketball Championships along with a Boys Maryland State Track and Field Championship, and a couple of Christian Private School Varsity Boys and Girls Basketball Championships.

High School basketball Coach Dr. Kevin Wilson Sr. with his 3 Maryland State Championship Basketball Rings

In his tenure as Head Coach and Assistant Coach, three dozen of his players became Division one basketball players, as well as a few who ended up as NBA and NFL players.

Dr. Wilson Is currently the high school and middle school Head Track and Field Coach for the Southern Maryland Christian Academy in White Plains, Maryland

Coach Dr. Wilson giving speech at the Southern Maryland Christian Academy Awards Banquet

He is certified in several areas in sports and has been for over thirty years. He is National Federal High School, Maryland and Virginia certified in coaching and officiating basketball and track and field, certified National Youth Sports Coaches Alliance Level 1,2,3, and 4, USATF and AAU certified official and basketball coach.

Coach Dr Wilson: USATF Official

Amongst his many achievements, Dr. Wilson has coached well over a thousand kids and made his way to becoming the founder and CEO of Wilson Basketball Incorporation (WBI). WBI trains kids from ages six to eighteen in the fundamentals of basketball and track and field. Dr. Wilson also currently partners with Fitness owners, John and Tammy Wright of the ABC Fitness connect in Waldorf Maryland which specializes in Fitness and Nutrition for Adults and Kids. The name of their venture is ABC/WBI Youth Conditioning Fundamentals Dr. Wilson is also a member of a Gospel singing Group the Committed Sons led by his brother-in-law Rodney Roach. Dr. Wilson has held over fifteen jobs in his life starting from the age of thirteen.

Committed Sons Gospel Singing Group

Not only that, but Dr. Wilborn is also a proud member of the Ark of Safety Christian Church in Upper Marlboro Maryland headed by Bishop C. Muse and First Lady Pat Lawson Muse, where he is on the Usher Board, Church Choir, and in the Church Drama Club headed by President/CEO and up and coming actor, director, writer, and visionary Dennis Jones.

Coach Dr. Wilbon Motivational Speaker Certification

Preface

Coach Dr. Kevin Wilson Sr

Success – it's a subjective term but most commonly associated with career and money. For me, success is growth; it's the essence of pushing your limits and becoming better. It's how I managed to study and receive five different degrees. Most people believe that there's an element of privilege often associated with career success. I, on the other hand, am a believer of hard work. It was a concept instilled in me by my parents, Phyllis Elizabeth Brooks Wilson and Calvin Wilson Jr.

My name is Coach Dr. Kevin Wilson Sr., and this is my story...

Contents

Dedication _____ i

Acknowledgment _____ iii

About the Author _____ ix

Preface _____ xvii

Chapter 1 _____ 1

Chapter 2 _____ 4

Chapter 3 _____ 10

Chapter 4 _____ 20

Chapter 5 _____ 25

Chapter 6 _____ 29

Chapter 7 _____ 40

Chapter 8 _____ 48

Chapter 9 _____ 56

Chapter 10 _____ 79

Chapter 11 _____ 84

Chapter 12 _____ 107

Chapter 1

"Start where you are. Use what you have. Do what you can."

Arthur Ashe

It was a warm afternoon when I lay in my mother's arms, cooing as I looked up at my dad. At the time, my brothers, Richard Bernard Wilbon and Darryl Anthony Wilbon sat close by. My mother often told me that I was always a happy baby, that I had smiled the moment I opened my eyes. I guess it was that happiness that carried with me throughout my life. I have a half-sister, Rebecca Yule. I found out about her later on and she was the same age as I was. Much later, I would have my other siblings – Calvin, Sharon Denise, and Sean Anton Wilbon – join the family. So, in total, we were about five brothers and two sisters.

As I grew to become more aware of the world, I could see the lifestyle we used to lead and absorb everything from my observations. One of the main things I saw was the struggle my parents went through. Regardless of the troubles, they managed to provide their kids with the best.

Mom was a school teacher and cook, while dad was a custodian. Both of them took their jobs seriously and ensured that we were always given the best of everything we wanted. Nothing stopped them from raising us right. My mom was always around; she was the woman who instilled her beliefs into us. Dad, on the other hand, would often come home from work when we were already asleep. I was still quite close to him, but we didn't have him around as much as mom.

Of course, we were all very close; it was my mother's religious and family beliefs that built us all up and united us.

"You can never leave your family behind," she would always say, and she was right. If there's anything I've learned, it's that family are the people who will stick with you throughout your journey. They're the ones you can rely on

1

when you have no one. Them, and your religion, are the two powers that never really part from you.

As kids, we were all pretty close-knit, always going out to play hide and seek, tag, etc. We were all about ten months apart, which made us connect better. Even today, we're all just as close and ensure that our kids, and their kids, learn the importance of family values as well.

Growing up, I saw my parents put their all into raising us; we watched them struggle day in and day out to provide us with a life where we were comfortable and happy. My mother, especially, was rather strict when it came down to it – she was our friend, but she was also the disciplinarian when she had to be. There was nothing we could do to escape her wrath, but at the same time, we knew that we could rely on her whenever we came across any problems.

Mom was the whooper – if you did something wrong, you always should be prepared for a whooping. It always started from the eldest, coming all the way down to the youngest. Sometimes, if she were too tired, she would let me off the hook and send me off to sleep. However, that never meant I was actually off the hook; you best believe that whenever I woke up, I would get the whooping I deserved!

My mom was a beautiful, loving person who cared about everyone. She was the best cook and everyone would come from everywhere to eat her food. She would feed anyone and everyone and there were time when our house would be crowded with people longing for her cooking. Daddy was a stern, serious, no-nonsense type of man. He didn't even have to whoop us if we did anything wrong, just the look on his face and his strong voice was enough to scare us. He was an excellent dresser with style and charisma and had a fondness for jewelry and the best smelling cologne. My dad always had the latest cars that was out and had a love for big cars like Cadillacs, Electric 225's and Lincolns Town Cars.

As far as me and my personality, I was a people-pleaser, and I loved making people laugh. It was the one thing that brought me joy, and it was something I inherited from my mom. Mom was a very loving woman, and she loved to laugh. She had a smile that could light up the room, and all my ability to joke and make people laugh came from her. She would joke a lot and always gave us the attention we needed. I never let go of that habit, though; I still love to help out anyone in need.

My mom was always there, telling me what a good job I was doing. She also loved music; every now and then, she would turn on the music and we would all start dancing, matching her love for it. She would play music when she was cleaning up on the weekends or doing the everyday chores.

The paramount lesson I learned growing up was the power of religion. Mom raised us to believe in God, Jesus Christ. The concept stuck with us throughout our lives because I came to know that nothing is possible without the Lord. I made a habit of praying every day and ask the Lord to sustain me. We were regular church-goers. My dad worked at St. Paul's Episcopal Church on 24th Street in Northwest Washington D.C., and he would take us there a couple times in the week to assist him. He was the head custodian who introduced us to Father Richards; his boss and the head clergyman of that church.

The church really took care of us, and they definitely loved my dad. It was amazing to see, really, and when I look back at it all now, I realize how much everything helped shape my life.

Most people don't realize that not everything falls on your lap; you have to work hard to achieve it, and given your circumstances, the effort you put in changes for everyone. Life is unpredictable, but what we lack now is our commitment to ourselves and the effort we put in for a change.

Chapter 2

Success is the sum of small efforts - repeated day in and day out.

Robert Collier

For most people, childhood is a relevant term to freedom – freedom from responsibilities, freedom from life's burdens, and freedom from adulthood. You're free to your innocence until your circumstances start affecting it. In my case, my surroundings were such that my freedom defined how I could make my life better. I put the responsibility on myself from an early age, and I always believed it came inbuilt for me.

Life in D.C. was anything but easy – the challenges were great, but it was something I knew I could work with and manage. One of the biggest challenges for me at that age was going to school and looking at kids and their cool toys. I was only human, after all, and a child at that – I was tempted to the same things they were.

However, it wasn't just the kids in school – it was also at home. We lived in a house with five families, and they all came from different backgrounds. While some were not so well off, the others had enough to afford good things for their children. We were in the middle, and when we looked at all the great things kids would get, we automatically had felt the difference between their and our situation. My siblings and I wanted good things too. However, my parents worked all the time, and they tried their best to provide us with enough.

Kevin Wilson at 10 years old

Then, whenever I would head off to school, I would watch kids eat their expensive candies, and my mouth would fill with saliva. My after-school routine was the same – I would head to the nearest candy store and eye all the candies there. I would stare at all the brown, pink, and blue candies with my puppy dog eyes while the cashier waited for me to order. Instead, I would look away sadly and head out the door with only one thing in my mind; I had to get my hands on them!

So, while all the other kids my age were waiting on their parents to get them good things, I decided to take matters into my own hands.

Seeing my parents tired at the end of the day only made me realize how much I couldn't ask them for candies or toys. And that marked the beginning of my hustler life. I didn't do anything bad or illegal, of course. However, to get what I wanted, I decided I had to earn it myself – it was my mom who had taught that to me. She was the one who had constantly taught all of us that nothing came for free. If we wanted candy from her, we would have to do the chores first. Slowly, as my siblings and I grew, we grasped the concept of working for what we needed. That's exactly what helped me then.

I was only seven years old, and my mind was stuck on those blue and pink treats. One day, I worked up the courage and marched right into a store, demanding a job. I say "demand" when I really mean that I politely asked the store clerk if there was any work that I could do. I was ready for anything – I asked if I could sweep around the store, carry bags, or even bag the items to afford the candy. It was in my eyes – the hunger I had for work. It was also my first experience in hustling.

It wasn't always easy, though. We lived on fourteenth street, and it was full of bad things going on. There were murders, prostitutes, and pimps on every corner. Everybody was out there trying to do whatever they could to get money. That would have been influential at my age, but my mother's teachings played a major role in guiding my hand. Whenever I had something on my mind, or problems I had to deal with, I had my entire family on my side – we were all very close, owing especially to our age differences.

Overall, though, the house was amazing – it was always chaotic and fun. There were always women in the house – my grandmother, aunts, mom, and cousins – and they always cooked and had fun. On the other hand, my grandfather was a construction worker and would make ice cream from scratch for us.

Generally, we all made the most of our time at home regardless of our financial conditions. I hold those memories close and ensure that my kids, too, face the same togetherness we did.

When it came to money, though, we're very better off now. Back then, when I wasn't working at the store, I found other ways to make money. Simply being at the store wasn't enough, I had my eyes on so many things. My brother once came up with the idea, and it was a good one too – my siblings and I would often head down to the laundromat for it. Here, people would often forget that they put quarters in the machine. We would go down there to see if I could get those quarters for the candy. More than the candy, I think we did it because it was fun.

Being a close-knit family, we made many memories – yes, we fought, but we all had a connection we couldn't let go of even as we grew older. Even as times changed and we let go of that big house and neighborhood and moved to Georgetown, our relationship never weakened.

Life was taking a turn, and as we settled into our new home, I started going to Stevens Elementary School on 21st Street. Our house was on 25th street, and I remember the beautiful quiet mornings. It was so different from our old house – there was safety and peace. Unlike before, we weren't in the ghetto anymore, we had moved to a nicer neighborhood.

This area was called Foggy Bottom, and it was absolutely beautiful!

There were times I would wake up in the morning and revel in the silence that surrounded our little neighborhood. I heard kids' laughter as they walked outside. There were no blaring horns, or any obnoxiously loud noise. This was one of the best neighborhoods to live in – mostly Caucasians lived here, or could afford to live there. It was just the better side of living.

I went to elementary school from the first to sixth grade, and there was so much that happened then. One of my fondest memories, though, was of Miss Coan – she was one of my teachers, and I had a major crush on her. I marveled at her beauty and how she taught in class. Rather than being a distraction, my crush led me to focus more on her class.

Miss Haliburton in the first grade, Miss Bolden in the second, Miss Williams in the third, Miss Lewis in the fourth, Miss Coleman in the fifth grade and Miss Coan in the sixth grade were all the teachers that I remember well because they all impacted my life. They knew the art of teaching, and their words helped in shaping my life. All of them held a message for me, and more than their words, it was their actions that I paid close attention to.

All of them gave me something to hold on to – there was a certain hope I felt when I went to class. My gym coach, especially, helped me out. His name was Mr. Russell, and he was the one to show me a side to my own life that I hadn't seen. Now, I was a short kid with a passion for basketball. However, I never aimed for it because I was always conscious of my height.

"Man, you are so short to be so fast. Maybe one of these days, you may be able to run track or, you know, play some basketball," Mr. Russel said to me. I was in the fifth grade then, and it sparked something in me – hope. I found that a lot at Georgetown; I aimed to be a go-getter, and the hope that I saw within myself only helped me better my focus in life.

I was still young, and my taste for good things only grew when I moved to this neighborhood. I saw more kids with things well beyond what my parents could afford.

This time, it was the school that motivated me to be independent. I had a love for wandering around, and I would end up doing several odd jobs to afford the things I wanted. I often found myself wandering down to Watergate, and there working at the Safeway I would bag groceries for people and make money.

When I was around nine or ten, I ran into several celebrities, whom were the Chilites and the Jackson Five. I was on top of the world! For a minute I thought I was dreaming, carrying the groceries up to the Chilites room and when they asked me to go to the show with them, I all but squealed with joy right then. I ran home that day, bursting in through the door, unable to contain myself. I would actually be going in a limousine with them too!

"There's no way you're going to go," my mom told me, immediately making my face drop. We had an argument, and I was sent to my room, but I later understood why she had stopped me; I didn't have the proper clothes to dress up for it as far as my mom was concerned.

I still never gave up my hope; I knew things would get better someday and that I wouldn't have to worry about things like this. However, back then, I made it all work one step at a time. This prompted me to go out and look for other employment opportunities and I would go where I knew money would be. I found myself wandering around Georgetown and ran across help wanted signs at several businesses. Gathering all the hope I had, I went into those businesses to see if I could get hired. Also, I got hired to hand out cards to people for a Palm Reading shop and the more cards I handed out, the more money I made.

It wasn't much but I did it because I wanted the extra cash. After doing that for months I got tired of it and I began looking elsewhere. Finally, I ended up working at a pizza place called the Black Olive which was also located in Georgetown. I loved Georgetown because of all stores, the glitz and glamour and it seemed as though this was the place to be even though, at my age, I had no business being up there. If my parents knew I was up there they'd kill me — so to speak. But after school that would be the place that I would frequent.

Chapter 3

A successful man is one who can lay a firm foundation with the bricks others have thrown at him.

David Brinkley

After a while, it was time for me to attend Jr. High School and life began to take a rapid change. After a lot of searching in the new area, we tried Francis Jr. High – from the outside, it seemed pretty great and I hoped it would be the same inside. When I began going there, I was pleased to find that it met my expectations.

My life was now beginning.

Kevin Wilson at 12 years old

This time, I knew that every decision I made would help me build my future and shape my life, but I was still a kid and the seriousness of it all hadn't yet settled in me. This was the time when my interest in basketball grew – Mr. Westmore was my coach, and he was an amazing coach. He was hard, firm, and tall – about 6'5'' and a very stern man, but you best believe he could play. The man was the best basketball player I had met, and with him as coach, a lot of the kids at that school already were pros. When I joined, I definitely lagged, but I never took that as my defeat. It was something I wasn't ready to do; not yet anyway.

Whenever I stepped into the court, kids would stare at me, expecting me to mess up so they could have a laugh. Instead of giving up, I moved forward and absorbed everything I was taught. Eventually, I made the basketball team at Francis. I was accustomed to the game and, for a moment, felt it truly defined me. I would go out every now and then, basking in the afternoon sun as my hands gripped the ball. I would often go and play on the other side of 25th Street, which was a long road divided into two, and situated right amidst of the urban neighborhood. Every day, my brothers and our friends would walk there, laughing over the going on's of life.

25th street was great – there was so much to do there. There were recreation centers, parks, basketball courts, and so much more. It was the hub of activities and, for a kid my age, it defined heaven. It was actually divided into two – the good side and the bad side. The good side – you guessed it – had a lot of well-off families living there. Most of them were associated with the military and so had a decent enough living. As for us, we worked our hardest to afford living there.

Life was more or less working out. School was fine, and I was holding on to everything I learned from my coach. When I reached seventh grade, my basketball skills had significantly gotten better. Where before I didn't get along with most of the kids, I was now reaching the center of attention, and I figured it was a great way to make money. It's not like there were any less tournaments there, and I got the opportunity.

The tournaments only honed the skills I had learned, and I also got to meet a lot of great guys there too. The boys I played with were really nice and, eventually, I became really good friends with them. We were a group of five boys, and some of the best players.

We would often meet on the 25th street, which was the good side of the neighborhood. Since Francis high school was on the bad side, we would have to walk there.

It was a whole lot of fun with these guys; we would go to rec centers and parks. We also went to talent shows and play summer league basketball teams in Georgetown. One time, I noticed that there were kids from the Bolling Air Force Base coming to Francis high school to play basketball. They seemed to be pretty good. I would often watch them – they would come to school every few weeks later.

So, one day, one of my friends decided he was going to sneak onto their bus because he wanted to mess with the girls and find out how they were living. I think that was the most fascinating thing. It was an eye-opener, really, looking at all the luxuries they had.

Eventually, I ended up joining one of their teams but got kicked out when I was caught. It was still fun though; we all had a ton of fun but also learned something or the other. It was a blissful escape from life's struggles.

Regardless of everything, basketball was the one constant in my life. Through all the troubles we were facing, I still found solace in the steady thud of the ball against the ground. The amazing part was that I actually learned from a girl back when 'sporty girls' were looked down upon. Of course, as a child, all I wanted to do was learn, regardless of what society had to say. I would often come by to help my father. It was there that I met a girl named Evette; she went to the school where my father worked, "The Immaculate Conception Academy," or ICA. Evette played basketball for the team at the ICA and was a superb player. I was mesmerized by how she dribbled, how she would run with the ball, stretching up over the hoop. She was about 6'2", and I was still an infatuated kid, especially with her game. Every time I would go around, she would throw the ball at me, challenging me for a game. She was the one who actually help refined my game and taught me how to do a lot of things that I couldn't have possibly imagined – every time I would go there, I would end up on the court with a ball in my hand.

I was already interested in sports, but I gained a much more profound love for the sport after watching her. Then began my journey to adulthood. While my parents worked for making our lives easier, I enjoyed sports and made sure I was making their lives easier.

When things began to go from bad to worse, though, sports wasn't my main concern anymore. I still worked up in Georgetown when I wasn't helping my father at the Church or ICA. My father had my brothers come to help him, so we took turns helping him out when he summoned us to be there. Often, I would go down to the Kennedy Center with my mind only on the money. This wasn't about convenience but survival. I was trying to make my life here and afford things I normally couldn't.

Kennedy Center was the hub of activities. I would go there with my friends, or sometimes with my siblings and, together, we would carry out various odd jobs. We would occasionally pick up trash and, other times, make money doing meagre work.

However, it wasn't all bad. I caught the biggest break of my young life when I went into a movie theatre named "The Biograph." I met a man named John Waters, who was intrigued by how I talked and my demeanor. He asked me why I was there at that theatre.

"I love movies, sir, and I want to see the animated movie "Heavy Traffic.""

I didn't know that it was a movie for adults only.

"Well, I'm sorry, but I can't let you go in and watch it," he laughed.

I left then, but it wasn't the end of our interaction. After talking to him for a while and stopping past to see him on several occasions, he ended up giving me a job there. John was an inspiring movie writer and told me that, one day, he would be famous as a movie writer, producer, and director. I believed him because I saw how he worked. He never sat idle; every time I would pass by, he was always writing. I would invite my brothers, cousins, and friends to the Biograph and let them in for free. I would give them free candy, popcorn, and drinks. Although it wasn't free, they still were impressed that I had that kind of pull there. John Waters told me that because of my attitude, the pursuit of making money, and willingness to work hard, I was a special person and one day be successful.

He taught me different things about making money and saving it for the future. He was a serious man on a mission, and it made me focus more on what I wanted in life. I appreciated everything he told me and will never forget it.

I appreciated that he was the first person to give me a chance at a proper job. It was mainly because of that that I was able to wander around Georgetown, knowing all the good places for work. He gave me that opportunity, and I'd be forever grateful.

Right after that, I got a job at a store called the Jean Jack, selling jeans, coats, and shoes. There was a guy named Vernon who worked there, and he was the one to offer me that job. From then on, the opportunities simply began to grow. I was hustling and making it through life, ensuring I relied on no one.

As time went on and we grew even more financially constrained, it began taking a toll on my parents and us. Eventually, we saw that Georgetown no longer had anything left for us. So we had to move into my grandfather's house over to NE DC. My grandfather, Thomas Phillips Brooks, my mom's father, was a man of principle and convictions who had steep and stern rules. I knew we wouldn't like being there, especially until my father figured something out. Granddaddy was a cab driver who spanned over fifty years and made a good living for himself doing so. He knew everyone, and he knew his way around the DMV area. I guess that's where I get my love for traveling and wandering around the area.

At my grandfather's house, you couldn't even say "dang" because it sounded too much like "damn" to him, and you couldn't say "shoot" because it

14

sounded too much like "sh**" to him. So, we knew we were in for it being cooped up over there on third and K street NE. Undoubtedly, all the back and forths were too much for a child, so I focused more on school to keep myself busy. However, moving in at my grandfather's house meant that we had to move again, and I would change schools.

Change is never easy, but they tend to take a darker turn when you're at the age I was. It seemed as though we were back where we started living on 14th and Newton Street NW DC because we were living with our uncles. All of us were sleeping in the basement at our grandfather's house. We were back at square one, sharing a home with my aunt Edna and uncles Pee Wee, Shug, Tiny, and our cousin, Butch, who would sometimes stay there. Each of my uncles were unique in their own way; Pee Wee spent time in the Marines and, unfortunately, got wounded and had to have his leg amputated. This led him to drink excessively, and he would have us run to the liquor store to get him stuff all the time. He was fun to be around for the most part, singing and writing love poetry and always asking me how to spell certain words to put in his poetry. Tiny is another story entirely that I'll talk about later. Shug was a cool, calm guy who loved to pull pranks on people and tease them to make everyone laugh; he was always pleasant to be around.

Aunt Edna was my grandfather's sister, she was old and seemed bitter but sweet at times, and she would drink a lot as well. Uncle Shug would tease her in front of us and make us laugh. My cousin, Butch, was my Uncle Sonny Boy's son; he was a pretty boy with a good physique. He was cool and always calm. We liked having him around; he would always wrestle my Uncle Tiny every time they got together for some reason or another. I guess that was their way of proving who was stronger between the two. I also had a cousin named Jose, who was definitely my biggest influence and was a man of the streets who everyone knew from every part of Washington DC. He was cool, could dress, and always kept money in his pockets; I definitely wanted to be like him. I would see Jose in Georgetown all the time, and he would ask me, "what are you doing up here? You should be home playing sports or something."

Jose taught me all the ins and outs of the streets and how to make money and not get into trouble. I learned everything I knew about street life from Jose!

Nevertheless, Georgetown had always been my escape – I grew accustomed to the routine, the people, and the life I had. I transferred from Francis junior high to Terrell junior high, which was in the Northwest, but my granddaddy lived in the Northeast. The walk there was through a tunnel, and it was in a terrible area – one surrounded by killings, drugs, and all the bad things you could imagine. Life got tough, it took a turn I didn't appreciate but didn't have much say in either. A part of me knew this was important for us, but another part of me hated it.

This was where I would come across kids who would significantly impact my life. As teenagers, we're all accustomed to thinking that we're always right, that our way is the only way. However, what happens when we take it to our heads? It wasn't something I had to wonder about because I began to live it.

I was never scared of going down that road to school, but it always bothered me. I hated having to face it because, like many other things, there were bullies all around. This one guy, Darnell, would specifically fight with me almost every day. It had become a routine – wake up, brush your teeth, get dressed, fight with Darnell, study at school. There was no way out. However, the fights didn't last long because he knew I wasn't scared of him and, to my surprise, that impressed him. Eventually, we did reach a consensus. Over time, though, the more I got to know him, the better friends we became. Darnell was unlike anybody I had hung out with. While he was a good fighter, he also revealed a side of me I wasn't particularly proud of. Darnell wasn't afraid of anything – he was a man of the streets. Anything you name, he was doing it. He was the polar opposite of me and had ended up becoming my friend. Mom didn't like it because I, too, was changing. From being the guy who was always careful and academically prevalent – to turning into the guy completely letting everything go, she began to worry. I was getting into things I had never done before; she wasn't happy with what she saw. I began to talk different, walk differently, and even behave differently. After a while, guys started to become jealous of me because of the popularity of hanging out with Darnell, but trust and believe that's not the best popularity to have hanging over your head.

Mom always told me not to hang out with him; she sensed trouble the day I disagreed with her, and it had begun a flurry of a constant storm within the house. My grandfather even weighed in on my mother's sentiments about how I needed to leave Darnell alone. For a while, things became hectic in my life.

Eventually, I began to transform. I didn't shoplift, but I would be 'the watcher.' I was assigned tasks like, "could you keep an eye on the owner while we steal this shirt?"

I agreed because I wanted to be there with them, but all I cared about then was that at least I looked good at the end of the day. I knew it was wrong, but I liked the outcome – I got all the goods and the money without actually doing anything; it was great! I had expensive clothes and shoes as well as plenty of money in my pocket, boasting and doing things I had no business doing. Girls would flock around me because of how I looked and what I was wearing. Guys would want to fight me because of their jealousy and envy. I mean, just think; I looked good, had money, and could play basketball as good as anyone my age and some older, so the jealousy and envy came with that territory. I loved the attention, not knowing that it had consumed me for all the wrong reasons. Often, it made me think of Uncle Tiny.

Uncle Tiny, who spent most of his life in and out of jail and had everyone terrified of him, always hit me up for money. Tiny would check my pockets and shoes to see if I was holding out and who was I to say no to him? I loved Tiny, though, because he would do anything in the world for his family, and he'd protect us from anything and anyone. I can recall how, one day, I was down on H street by the Atlas theater, and some guys tried to jump and rob me. It was late at night, and I had no business being over on that end of NE. I ran all the way home, and who did I run into? Yes, my uncle Tiny! I told him what happened, and he took me back to where I ran from, and I pointed out the guys who had confronted me earlier. He beat every last one of them up.

These are some of the things that happen when you are in the streets like I was. Nevertheless, after all these things I was going through, common sense was lost to me until, one day, I got the news that the police arrested Darnell for shoplifting. I was at home when one of my friends came to pick me up. We were heading to yet another store.

"Where's Darnell?" I asked him because it was usually Darnell who picked me up.

"Man, he was caught. The police threw him in jail."

The blood drained from my body. I was terrified about what would happen if the police caught me. After all, I was still aiding the crime.

When I got home, I took a long, hard look at myself. I had become someone else, someone I didn't appreciate.

"That's it. No more," I thought then and put my mind to it. I couldn't see myself in jail; it wasn't the place for me. More than myself, I thought about my parents and how they would feel. I knew I couldn't stand facing my mother's disappointment; it would be too much to bear. But it was too late, my name was given to the authorities, and I had to turn myself to the police. They arrested me for being an accessory to shoplifting. This was my first arrest and a shock to me, and an embarrassment to my parents. I pleaded guilty and got off because it was my first time being charged with anything. My record had been clean up until now, plus they really didn't have anything on me. Everything is just hearsay. So, I was fortunate at that time.

I made amends without a second thought and returned to my old habit, and never looked back. I was back to shooting hoops, and I was good. I would head out to the courtyard every now and then and welcome the game like it was a long-lost friend. I had practiced before and had gotten so good over time I could easily play with Mr. Westmore, but I knew he would win. I was soon given the name "Cornbread" after the movie "Cornbread, Earl, and Me," starring Lawrence Fishburne.

I was short, but I was a good player, which eventually earned me the respect I had lost over time. I learned something then, something that I hadn't really paid attention to before – these pimps and the 'bad guys' we're surrounded with, they claim you. They claimed me too, but after I went back to basketball, they prevented me from doing the wrong things. They would keep me away from the terrible areas, give me money and clothes, and simply take care of me. It pushed me further to pursue basketball, and I would often play over at Hayes playground on 5th street.

Undoubtedly, I was the best player around. Regardless, it didn't fight out Darnell's influence on me. I did have an uncle that did have some influence in my life, and that was uncle Tony. I remember my uncle Tony coming to my grandma's funeral in his army uniform when I was young, which stuck out to me for life. He would sit down and talk to me about being responsible and doing the right things. He never criticized or judged me but always said to be accountable for my actions and know that my wrongful actions could have dire consequences. But how could I when things were so bad at home?

They had only grown rougher over the months until, one day, my dad came home with the news that we were moving to Maryland. Our struggles were now going to go down. With my dad getting his act together again, we were packing up for yet another move.

Chapter 4

"However difficult life may seem, there is always something you can do and succeed at."

Stephen Hawking

Life was going in a direction I could learn to appreciate over time. Moving to Maryland was a significant change in my life and a fresh start that, I believe, the entire family needed. With the direction I was going, it was only a matter of time before I would fall back into the practices, I was trying my best to let go of.

Grandad's house in the Northeast was all about convenience. He was a cab driver and ensured that we were all taken care of – the other uncles we lived with and us. We had uncle Tiny, uncle Slug, uncle Pee Wee, and my cousin Butch – and out of all of them, Uncle Tiny was quite the piece of work. The man was always in jail, and you couldn't mess around with him. However, he was amazing. If we needed anything, we knew uncle Tiny would be there. He always had our backs and would beat up anyone who crossed him. I always appreciated him for protecting us and often visited him in jail. It was always nice to have Uncle Tiny around. With him, there were no problems I couldn't face.

A change in my parents' jobs came with a major change in our lifestyles as well. Where we had become accustomed to relying on my grandfather for the basic things, we would now become self-sufficient. We no longer had to wait for him to take out money from the closet for us. It's not like he minded; he loved taking care of us. Regardless of how terrible living in the Northeast was for us, my grandfather and uncles made it worthwhile.

Our house in Maryland was a double step up from my grandfather's house in the Northeast. It was much bigger, and for the first time in a long time, I wouldn't have to face the gangsters lining the walk to school, and that, in itself, felt like a blessing. When we drove into the neighborhood, my eyes widened at how perfectly organized everything was. It was a stark contrast to our neighborhood before. All the houses were the same; they were all perfectly aligned. The grass in their yards was green, and the trees lining the pathways cast soft orange hues of sun rays falling on them. Where we were accustomed to the noise and beaten down, old homes, here, we were moving past newly built homes in a quiet neighborhood.

However, nothing came without its own set of problems. Ours was mainly racism. Wheaton, the place where we moved to, was a predominantly white neighborhood. As we passed by in our car full of bags and the kids all clinging to the windows, I couldn't help but notice the stares. Most people there were white, and they watched us as though we didn't belong. I noticed how some would look at us and then amongst themselves as though questioning what we were doing there. I didn't think much of it then, but I realized that this was something I would better understand later in life. Wheaton had major segregation between the races. There weren't many black families on our street, which meant facing our fair share of troubles. However, it wasn't just the neighborhood I had a problem with; it was also the school. When I attended Belt Junior High, I felt out of place. It seemed like I was the only black kid in a sea of white faces, including the teachers. There were other black kids too, but they were a handful of them.

I was ignored for most of my first month there, and the second month onwards was when the fights began. I would get in a lot of conflicts with the white guys. It was evident – they didn't want my siblings or me there, but we weren't going to leave either. I was able to deal with it, though, my attitude was a little different from most blacks who lived there. Growing up in an urban neighborhood gave me enough chances to change. The blacks who were actually born there were completely different from our family.

I wasn't the prejudiced type – if I felt as though someone didn't like me, then I would steer clear of them. I wasn't the type to hold anything against people. I didn't want to be the type of person to hold grudges or make enemies. However, people themselves tried to fight me then there was nothing that I could do about it.

Things weren't all bad, though; apart from learning self-control, I also got a job working at Miss Harper's distribution and cooperation in Rockville, Maryland. It was a company that distributed boxes full of clothes, and I was in charge of boxing them up in the warehouse. I would also do the invoices. While it wasn't really what I was interested in, I was making enough money to manage my own expenses while also learning the tricks of the trade. It was the growth that formed the basis of my career growth. I went on to hold various of others jobs like Farrell's Ice Cream Parlor, Little Tavern, and Sunoco Gas Station, just to name a few that I started out with.

Eventually, junior high ended, leading me to Wheaton high school. I finally got to play basketball again without having the entire yard against me. However, my priorities then were completely different. I wasn't looking for just a couple of hoops but rather money. I wanted to start earning some real cash, and this passion led me to flourish the most. I was playing basketball, running track, and simply taking up a lot of sports. One year, I played football, and I was the fastest kid on the field and the smallest.

I got hit hard one time in a game, and that was when I knew I was done. I decided that I wasn't playing anymore, but the problem was that my football coach was also my basketball coach.

"Kevin, you need to get out there and do something else, he told me after one of the games. I returned from the game with my jersey tucked under my arms, and the bag pack hung loose. I looked at him standing by the bleachers and looking out at the other kids, then turned his attention back to me.

"You can't be a one-sport person. Expand your horizons," he told me. I looked out into the field at the kids kicking the ball around and sighed. I knew he was right.

I took my time thinking about it, and after surveying my options, I concluded that I was going to run track. It seemed like the best thing to do. However, there was something inside of me that still wasn't satisfied. I was always a basketball fan, and simply letting that go wasn't easy – it was my calling, after all.

Wheaton was a much-needed fresh beginning to a whole new life. I ended up making a whole lot of friends. I met them through basketball, and they were truly a fresh breath of air from the people I had come across all through my time at Wheaton. We always had a great time – we would get together after school and go out. There were about six of us, and all of us would be meeting up to play against other people. It was a fantastic way to harness my skills while also doing what I loved. Over time, I grew from becoming the boy who simply lived life on a day-to-day basis to a man believing that things could get better. I understood that my life was my own, and so were my expenses.

Where I once used to hang out with people who stole to get easy money, I was now earning my own. I was building my own future, regardless of the hurdles that crossed my path.

No matter how much I ran track, it still didn't compare to basketball – my sanctuary. Finally, I ended up playing varsity basketball.

But it wasn't just sports; Wheaton opened up a ton of opportunities for me. I first got a job at McDonald's – I worked in the kitchen flipping burgers. It paid for everything I needed, and that was all I cared about. Once I got out of that, I joined Pharaoh's Ice cream parlor. My opportunities just continued to grow. I think my favorite job was the one I got at Athlete's Foot – a sports store that sold shoes. I would be so excited to go there, and every time I would enter, I would be greeted by the soft scent of leather. I missed the job when I left, mainly because I loved looking at the shoes. However, I felt as though I had fulfilled my time there. I moved from there with my brother, and the two of us joined Bloomingdales in the 11th grade. You see, they had a restaurant and, at that time, Richard and I applied for a job there.

And it was that effort that ended up helping me get my own first car. It was when everyone I knew in school had a car. It was the thing that made you a big shot. I ended up buying a Mercury Marquis, and my father was not happy.

"You're too young to own a car, Kevin," my father said, but I was old enough to know better – or so I thought. As it turned out, luck wasn't really by my side. Much to my disappointment, I didn't have that car very long. After having my car for only a few days, the unexpected happened. One day, while going to pick up my oldest brother Richard from work at Bloomingdale's at White Flint Mall in Rockville, where we both worked, I was in my own zone, oblivious to the trouble lurking around the corner when, suddenly, out of nowhere, another car came speeding towards me, wrecking into my car. The loud boom resonated in my head, and my car spun; I could have been sent flying out, but I was wearing my seatbelt and sustained minor injuries. My car, however, was totaled, and just like that, it was gone; I fractured my ribs and had a concussion and had to be rushed to Holy Cross Hospital.

All I cared about, though, was that at least I got to try it. I owned my own car, regardless of how short period of time it was for, and I ended up getting the best of it. I wouldn't say that it was to impress girls, but it sure did attract a lot of attention. Wheaton high school was the hub of guys trying to woo their girlfriends by exceeding the amount of money their parents had. I always thought that my car would get me that same attention, and boy, was I right! I ended up getting a girlfriend, but that relationship didn't last very long.

Regardless, everything I did till then was about self-sustenance. I never wanted to rely on anybody to do things for me. I always wanted to rely on myself, and I did. I guess that's the main point; to better understand your potential, you need to push yourself to what you can achieve.

Chapter 5

"However difficult life may seem, there is always something you can do and succeed at."

Stephen Hawking

By the time I reached 17th grade, adulthood had made its way to me. I was no longer a kid making rash decisions, but rather, I was a man dealing with the consequences of my past decisions. By now, I was looking into colleges I could join, and my attention was on George Mason University. The problem was that I had no funds.

I had worked for so long but managed to save nothing, and that decision was now coming back to bite me. I went through a work-release program in the 12th grade, which meant that I could take one class and work. I would still be getting the credit, and so, when I graduated, I had more credit than I needed but no funds to afford college. I was heartbroken; it was my chance at success, and I couldn't hang on to it.

The bad news was that my parents were broke too and couldn't afford me to go into George Mason. I had the offer in hand but no scholarship to go with it. It seemed like no matter which way I looked, college seemed to be a dead-end for me. It was the option that held no possibility for me. If I did go, I would drown myself in debt, and that wasn't something I was looking forward to. The more I tried to perceive my future, the more I lacked in understanding the path my life would take.

I looked around me and noticed that there was one thing I had forgotten — the military. Now, that was an option I simply could not miss out on. I remembered my uncle's words and how I felt every time he would visit, adorned in the military uniform. I was always in awe of him and the constant wisdom he would have for me.

At that moment, without a minute of hesitation, I was ready. I had already taken the ASVAB test in high school. Now, when I filled out the form, I was vaguely aware of how things were going to go. I was excited and on edge.

My parents were thrilled, though my mom did prefer that I didn't go. She wanted me home where she knew I was safe. My dad, on the other hand, couldn't care less. For him, it was just one less mouth to feed!

I had put my faith in God and trusted the decision I was supposed to make. My family had raised us to be strong, willing, and hard-hitting boys, and I took advantage of that to join the military. I felt as though it was a decision that God had helped me make to get away from the environment I was used to. I was built to grow, and if I didn't join the military, then I would miss out on it.

Joining the military wasn't a dream or luck. It was a decision I made purely due to the lack of options. I had dreaded going there, no matter how much I marveled at my uncle and all the other veterans I had come across. Regardless, I had heard the stories and knew just how difficult adjusting there would be. It was terrifying, especially thinking about getting out of my comfort zone. Regardless, it was either that or stay home and work meager jobs, and I was inclined more towards the former.

Pvt Kevin Wilson when he first joined the US Army 1981

The first week in the military, I was stumped. I was away from home and everything that I had once known, and I was forced to change my entire pattern of living. The change wasn't pleasant; it came with all the hardships you could imagine. It was so tough that, within a week, I called my mother and told her I was coming back.

"No, you're not. You don't have a bed here anymore. You're staying there and doing whatever it is you have to do there. You're not running when things get tough," she told me. At that moment, I was heartbroken and annoyed. However, I learned that that was the best advice I had received over the years. Her words got me through basic training, and I ended up excelling at practically everything. I had a voice telling me I could do it, which made me push myself. Those countless hours exercising under the blazing hot sun, listening to the sergeant's constant orders, the tasteless foods, and the horrific mental and physical stress. Throughout that time, I also saw a lot of the people I befriended give up and leave.

However, there was no way I could leave. I was being pushed to perfection and achieved things I would never have thought of before.

I believed that there was a lot I had to learn, and that would eventually help me if I ever decided to leave the military. I was right.

There are many things that people usually don't understand, the biggest of which is the concept of hard work. When you put your mind to something, no one can stop you from achieving it. That belief is what pushes people to give their best, and it's what allows them to see the bigger picture. This is what I learned throughout my life there; if I didn't have the motivation or vision for my life, I would never be able to put in the effort I did.

Chapter 6

*"The will to win, the desire to succeed, the urge to reach your full potential...
these are the keys that will unlock the door to personal excellence."*

Confucius

I remember I had once woken in the middle of the night drenched in sweat. I had dreamt of darkness, and there was nothing that I could see ahead. Then, suddenly, I saw something; it was beautiful, and I couldn't quite tell what it was. There was a feeling I had, though; it was a feeling of hope and that everything was going to be alright.

When I woke up surrounded by the same darkness, I almost screamed. But slowly, the freckles of light became visible as my sight adjusted to the night, and I saw the silhouettes of others lying on the beds not so far from each other. I was still at camp, and when I looked out the window, I saw the moon shining bright outside. It was hope – the same one I had lost.

"The Lord is there for you if you only wish to see Him guide your hand," my mother would always say whenever I found myself in a mess. This night, as the initial week of basic training passed, I could feel the Lord's hand guiding me. I smiled and laid back in bed, a renewed courage echoing in my heart. I wouldn't say I was built for greatness – nothing was easy for me. There were so many times when I wanted to give up, and this was one of them. I don't think I have faced hardships like I did in basic training, but I learned to take it one step at a time, and before I knew it, I was through! The exhilaration I felt was beyond belief. I had stood by and watched so many people give up, but there I stood, at the graduation with my head held high. Regardless, the journey wasn't over yet. Once I completed the training, I was on my way to becoming a squad leader. I was shipped off to Fort Lee, Virginia, The Army Quartermaster School for my (AIT), which stands for Advanced Individual Training to train me for my military occupation. The job that I'd be training for is called The Army Maintenance Management System (TAMMS). This meant that I would be working in the military motor pool as a dispatcher and supplier of vehicle parts for all types of vehicles for the military. The Army Quartermaster School trains soldiers for Logistics, Supply and Culinary Arts occupations.

SSG Kevin Wilson in the Army Stripes Paper in Nov 1991

I wasn't nervous, but I did wonder if I was able to cope with the life I had planned ahead. I knew that nothing went according to plan, but I still wanted to see where I would end up. As it turns out, I managed to become a squad leader in Fort Lee. It was a whole new experience, one that was brought on by the experiences I had in Fort Jackson.

In Fort Lee, we had a lot more leeway for the things we wanted to do, which wasn't allowed in basic training. It also meant that I met a whole lot of different people from all walks of life and different states and countries. I actually got to know people from places I had never even heard of, and each of them carried a different persona and a different attitude. It was very interesting, and it opened my mind to the kind of things I had yet to experience.

One of these happened right when I was stationed at Fort Lee. It was a company named the Whiskey Company. What happened was that the companies were named after the military alphabets from A-Z. For me, it happened to be 'W.' I had a commander there, by the name of Lieutenant Sua, who was a beautiful Hawaiian Lieutenant. She was a gorgeous lady – tall, thick, and beautiful. The best thing about her was that she didn't take any shit from anyone.

Now, the Whiskey Company wasn't a walk in the park. Even though I knew everyone there, and we were essentially doing the same job, it was still different.

My job initials were 76 Charlie, and that's what they would call me. It would take me back to basic training. The similarities were plenty – you still had to get up and do the physical training every day. You would have to run two miles and do your pushups then. There was only one difference, though; you didn't have to put the alarm for four in the morning.

The routine was set for seven in the morning – I would get up, do my physical training, get dressed, do half-formation and then go for my job. I was a little motivated since I had become the squad leader. However, I was determined to follow through with that.

After leaving the basic training, life had taken a whole turn – it was very difficult. The only good thing, I would say, was meeting different people. They managed to make it fun; it was actually one of the times when I actually felt free. We had liberty there – we could go to parties off base and do a lot of things. It was great, but there was still a lot of pressure on me.

Life was tough, and while I felt the progression in me, I still missed my family. You'd think I'd be accustomed to being away from them, but it only got worse. It had been a long time since I saw them – every morning, I would wake up to the memory of them standing outside the house and waving goodbye to me as Richard dropped me off at the station.

We weren't allowed to visit anyone in basic training, but we could talk to them. Now, however, I could visit them, especially on the three-day weekend we would get.

After the first few weeks of basic training, I made sure I set my new routine. After that, I began to look up train tickets home. Once I learned I was free to go anywhere I wanted, my heart soared with excitement. This was much-wanted freedom!

I booked the tickets, packed my bags, and was off after spending thirteen weeks in basic training. I looked out at the passing sceneries the entire ride home, hoping time would move faster. There was an eagerness that pushed me forward. I was awaiting a life I had lost.

What I hadn't realized was that I had changed. I had become a completely different person from when I had last left. The day I had reached basic training, I was just a young boy trying to take his place in the world. I was a thin kid who had basically given up on taking care of himself and only hoped for a better future.

Now, however, I was a man who had grown from the shackles that life had cast on me. I now had opportunities in front of me, and my physique had changed too. All that hard work in basic training helped me build my muscles and gain weight. My mind worked differently, too; I could feel it.

As I looked out of the window, I wondered what it would be like to return home. I was essentially returning as a different person – a more responsible person. I knew my parents would be proud, but how would they react? All of these thoughts itched in my mind.

I hadn't told anyone I was coming back home; it was meant to be a surprise. Hiding it was one of the most difficult things I had done, but I was excited, more so than anyone else could be. When the train stopped at the station, I jolted awake from my sweet slumber, and my heart almost leapt out of my chest – I was here.

I got up, picked up my things, stepped out of the train, and hailed a ride. I was heading home. The soft, pale moonlight followed me, hiding behind the yellow fluorescent street lights. Since it was Sunday, I knew everyone would be home. I made my way past the familiar streets and the neighborhood I had almost forgotten until the familiar brown house came into view. It was just as I remembered it – nothing had changed. I took a deep breath and stepped out of the cab.

"Thanks," I said and paid him. My feet refused to move even though I wanted to run. However, I was numb with excitement.

I took a breath and went on my way. My mom opened the door, and when she saw me, she screamed. Suddenly, everyone else was there, standing there in shock. It truly was – they could tell how much I had changed. The longer I stayed there, the longer I noticed how much respect I received. It was more than I had received in my entire life. They saw me as a whole new man – a mature, respected man. It wasn't just the physical aspects, but it was also the way I walked or talked. My entire personality had changed, and people were looking at me in a positive light. It felt good.

However, no matter how much I liked it, I couldn't really stay there. Home now felt a temporary resort from the real world. I often thought about home, but returning was something I couldn't deny. Eventually, when the time came, I bid everyone farewell and was on my way back.

Many things were going on when I rejoined AIT back at Ft. Lee, Virginia. I thought life was difficult in basic training; it turned out that it was so much worse now. Eventually, we had a skill training test in which we needed to score at least 90% or more for on a permanent station, and if we didn't, we could be recycled back for a different job or just kicked out.

It wasn't an option for me, and while I did try my best, I ended up being only three points away. It was frustrating, but since I was close, I didn't get kicked out, but I had to do remedial training. It felt like a setback – that regardless of how hard I tried, I still couldn't reach that point. I didn't give up;

I got another job ordering parts for vehicles. It wasn't as simple as it sounds – it meant that I had to look up catalogs and know different parts. They had skew, ISN, and serial numbers, which made it difficult. I wouldn't say that the work was exciting – it was anything but exciting, but it did help me down the road.

I aimed for a promotion, which I got later on down the road.

Life was very different in the army, and the more I progressed, the better I learned to stand up for myself. Moreover, the gain in rank came with a handsome pay increase which, in itself, was amazing. However, the PT tests that I had to pass weren't easy. There were things like doing a certain set of pushups in two minutes. You get different drill instructions. You also get real tug drill instructors and teachers, and the ones I got seemed to pick on me a lot. I figured it was because I came in as a PFC, and they wanted to know if I truly did deserve my rank.

Their preliminary test was whether or not I was able to lead people, and that, in itself, was challenging both mentally and physically. It felt as though all I did was work apart from the little times I got to do anything else. The fun was different from your average 'fun;' our company often held talent shows and competitions. Furthermore, we had basketball! I would play basketball for my company, and I loved how I still had it. I never had the goal of being a soldier, which was what pushed me forward.

I was the best player in the company, and everybody cheered for me. That was the one thing that kept pushing me forward and making me believe that I could achieve whatever I put my mind to. Whenever I had free time on my hands, I would head to the gym and practice basketball. It was one of the things that I felt like I was fortunate enough to pursue here. Now, I could see my life-changing for the better.

Before this, I always had doubts about my success. It bothered me that I wasn't able to go to college, and everyone I knew had reached the position I had dreamed of. Now that I look back at my life, I finally felt as though I was getting somewhere. I knew about the challenge and accepted it, and, eventually, it was paying off.

At least I got to play basketball, and that's something I truly appreciated. I didn't waste a single moment to play. The rest of the time I had, I would spend it reading a lot of different journals and perfecting my skills according to the job. While I knew whatever I had to know, I still needed to expand my knowledge. I had to know what I was going to do when I left, and this was a positive change for me. Eventually, I graduated at the top of my class.

It was a lot of hard work that I put in, and all of it paid off. After my promotion, my first orders were to go to Fort Bragg, North Carolina. When I reached there, I actually joined the HHC 16 MP brigade. It was the first company I joined. I was excited beyond belief. The best part was that I was finally out of the initial phase and had begun my job.

The job wasn't very different from what I had experienced before, but I did notice that a lot of people on the post wore berets. Most of the berets had a different color – some were green, some black, and some were burgundy. I didn't realize it then, but soon enough, I found that it was because of the different units.

The elite units wore green berets. We had rangers and airborne soldiers there, and if you wanted to wear the beret, you had to earn it. The things you had to do were tough. You see, I, too, was challenged to see if I was able to do any of that. However, I couldn't compare to those guys – they were big and strong, and you could tell that they worked out. They were the guys who went through a lot of training. Personally, my exposure to training was insignificant, but there was one time when I went through a post exchange. At this time, I could buy clothes, shoes, and even food for myself. At that time, we ran into these guys with black berets, and they looked at us for a minute.

"What're you looking at?" They asked, followed by a long line of insults. These guys were big, and we obviously couldn't say much to them because I knew they might be crazy. Later, I found out that these guys were Rangers, and, honestly, I was impressed. However, I knew that wasn't for me. No matter how impressed I was, I knew that that wasn't a position I could reach.

That's one of the most important things I learned, and I believe that others should learn too – don't try to overstep things you know you can't do. Of course, it's only better to try and know your own limitations. If you don't, you may end up in a position you don't want to be in.

I gave it a thought, though, the green berets looked damn good, and boy, did they act that way. However, I knew I couldn't push myself to that point; I only had so many limitations. I took my time in figuring out what I had to do, and I ended up signing up for airborne school. That was a dream – jumping out of airplanes always grabbed my attention. Now, it was time when I could learn it and not make it sound like a death wish!

Going into airborne school was like a dream come true. It was everything I had hoped for, and while it was tough, it was also a challenge I was willing to take up. We began by learning how to be riggers and then learnt to pack our own parachutes. It wasn't a game you learnt in just a couple of minutes. Rather, it was a six-week course. I didn't just work through it, but I also had to train for it.

The most important thing was ensuring that I was physically fit to be in airborne training. Now, from all of the training, I went through, this was probably the toughest one I had to endure.

That only meant one thing – graduating from airborne school was one of the proudest moments of my life. It took a while, sure, but I never gave up. Instead, I became airborne – a privilege that so few people get to witness.

This was the moment when I truly believed I could do anything I wanted to. All I had to do was put my mind to it, which is something that many people don't realize – a feat is only the test of potential. You will eventually succeed if you're willing to move ahead regardless of your situation. In this case, I didn't let anything stop me – not my lack of motivation, not the other people who quit, and not my internal monologue telling me I wasn't worthy enough for it.

I took the challenge dead on and became an airborne soldier. This was the thing that set me apart from the other guys, who were often called legs because their duty mainly required them to walk. For us, though, we flew. We jumped out of planes in the sky, and we soared like eagles landing on the ground. I was no longer a leg. After becoming airborne, I attended Air Assault School training at Ft. Campbell, Kentucky, learning how to propel up and down helicopters while dangling on the ropes in the air, which added another notch in my belt as a soldier.

I was amongst the most respected soldiers thereafter, I became airborne, and air assault, then got promoted to E-4, a specialist in the military. They also changed my job from 76 Charlie to 76 Yankee, which was logistics and supply. And I ended up becoming a supply specialist, which, to me, was a move up from the motor pool to the supply room.

While working in the supply room, there were a lot of other responsibilities that had to be met, and a lot of them fell on me. After being promoted, my supply sergeant wanted me to become the company's Nuclear Biological Chemical (NBC) specialist. I had to go to school to learn and train soldiers in my company. I graduated from the NBC course and proudly served that position in the company. Six months after that, I was tasked to be the Arms Room NCO, which is also a supply room function, especially being in a Military Police company.

I had a keen knowledge of weapons, taking them apart and putting them back together in record time and earned the Expert Shooting Badge in rifle shooting, hitting 39 out of 40 targets from 200 and 300 meters away. So, my qualifications for being an armorer for the company was justified. This looked good on my military record and gave me hopes of being promoted to a Sergeant once the promotion cycle comes back.

I received much respect in my company for taking on those jobs and responsibilities and passing the inspections that came around annually with high scores. This gave me more confidence that I could be a great leader as well as a supervisor amongst soldiers, and I was well ahead of my peers within the brigade.

I would say that I was more or less privileged – or at least I felt that way as I waited for my second duty assignment. I was there for two years, but I never missed the opportunity to learn my craft. The more I expanded my knowledge, the more I opened myself up to better opportunities until, eventually, I was able to get promoted. It felt amazing when I was able to make the post-basketball team there.

Basketball was the one thing that allowed me to get out of work a lot. It felt pretty great to know that I was able to do so much while being in the military – I had the chance to have fun and get paid, both simultaneously. It felt like a once in a lifetime opportunity.

However, one of the greatest moments was when I was able to afford a car. It was unbelievable. All I could think about at that point was how much I had struggled to buy my first car. Now, here I was, using my tax refund to buy myself a brand-new car and one I actually was hopeful for. It was all white with light blue on it and paid completely by myself!

When I visited home that weekend, I could see the jealousy everyone had. Initially, I would only depend on the rides I would get from my friends, Gene and Bullard, but now, I could drive myself. Gene had been very helpful, always ready to take me wherever I had to go. Now, I was my own person, and that was something to be proud of – I didn't have to rely on anyone; I could simply hop in the car and head to meet my mom and siblings whenever I wanted. I now had a sense of purpose in my life, which I had forgotten so long ago.

It wasn't just the car; it was the fact that I had matured so much in my life. I went from being an immature boy always getting in trouble to the experienced adult who people now came to for advice. I had a nice living situation and a nice car, I was doing very well overall, and I loved it.

Then, one time, my brother, Darryl, decided he wanted to visit me in Fort Bragg just to see how I was living. I lived in the barracks, but I had my own room. People would often sneak their friends in there for the night. It wasn't allowed, but that didn't really stop anyone.

I did the same; I drove my brothers, Darryl and Calvin, to the barracks. We first hit the club and then came back. The entire time, though, I couldn't help but wonder where they would stay. Let's face it, the room is big enough for one, maximum two people; not three.

I decided I would leave the car with them and take the bus. What could go wrong, right? The next time I went home on a three-day weekend, I had to pick up the car. Man, when I got it, it was unusable. I don't know what they did, but it wasn't working. I got so upset and vowed never to let anyone borrow my car again.

It was just one of the things I learned over time, but most of them the lessons were from the soldiers and their own lives. I absorbed them all, taking the lessons with me and applying it to my own life. I pushed forward because of those lessons and never allowed myself to adhere to anything lesser. I had a sergeant there; he was my first sergeant and a great guy!

Of course, owing to his role, he would chastise you if you ever broke the rules but never adhered to punishment. He was the guy who was always open to conversation; he would sit you down and tell you where you made a mistake and what you could do to rectify it.

"You learn from your mistakes only when you get back up and keep moving forward," he would always say and made sure we followed it.

Fortunately enough, though, the future was still at hand – my time at Fort Bragg had come to an end, and I was now looking forward to a whole new start in Korea.

Chapter 7

"If you are not willing to risk the usual, you will have to settle for the ordinary."

Jim Rohn

Here's the thing about life; it pushes you to circumstances you never thought you would be in. You'll be in situations that may seem near to impossible for you to comprehend, and yet, you'll be surprised at how you persevere.

My life had been a roller coaster ride from the moment I entered the military. I had to push myself to deal with things I never thought I would be able to – and yet, here I was. Korea was a whole new chapter of my life. The only problem was that Korea was colder than the temperature I was used to. I was a supply sergeant there, which meant that I had to go through several pick-ups and deliveries. It snowed when I was there, and the cold would reach straight to my bones. However, since I had to move around so much, it didn't take my body too much time to get used to it. Throughout the one year that I was there, we would go to the DMZ, which stood for the demilitarized zone. We couldn't cross to the other side from there because the war was going on.

It was overwhelming if I'm being honest. The constant rattle of gunshots and bombs had become a part of life, but it was one of the things I couldn't dismiss.

Worst of all was the food. I ate for survival and survival purposes only. I missed home and the foods that would leave us wanting more. Here, it was the kind that made my tastebuds scream at me for torturing them so. Regardless, it wasn't all bad – I did like the fact that you didn't have to go too many places to buy clothes. You could get practically any kind of clothes you wanted, and whatever you wanted made, they would make it for you. It was great!

I knew for a fact that if people back home saw the kind of things we had in Korea, they would only purchase things from there!

Korea was the kind of place where we simply could not take our family with us even if we wanted to. The only condition to see them as if they were in the military themselves. No one could take anyone there with them, and since it was my first duty station overseas, I missed my family terribly.

I often thought about them; about what they would be doing or how they might be living. I have to admit, it made my heartache. Although I met many different Korean people there, and they were very nice to me and treated me well, I guess I was just accustomed to the American lifestyle. At first, the transition hit me hard. I would prefer to stay by myself in my room. But then, eventually, the rest of the guys pulled me out of the depression I was slowly sinking in.

Korea made way for me to meet many different people, and I noticed a pattern – Koreans, in general, were very nice and helpful. They went beyond to make me feel comfortable as well. I think that was the major factor that helped my stay get better. There were also the women. Korean women are absolutely beautiful, and a lot of my friends ended up messing with or marrying them. I, on the other hand, wasn't very interested.

My focus was one thing and one thing only – self-growth. I wanted to ensure that I grew every day and became better at my game. So, while most of my friends were out partying, I would hit the court for a game or two.

There was something different about basketball in Korea; it didn't feel the same as it did in the states. I guess it was because I kept myself very aware of the fact that I wasn't there anymore. I tried not to, but it came naturally. Every time I played, it didn't matter how long it took for me to come and settle here; all I wanted was to go back home. One night, I made up my mind and promised myself that I would go somewhere close to Virginia when I went back home.

But, as I said earlier, none of your plans ever work out the way you want them to, and that's the beauty of life. Every time it gets you away from where you thought you would be, it shows you what was in store for you.

Once my year in Korea was completed, I was told that I would be sent to Germany, not back home. Something inside me broke that day – I missed home, but I had no choice. I thought about it a lot until I figured it out – I could always visit home before leaving. Yes, it wouldn't be the same as staying there, but at least it was something.

I packed up, booked my flight, and headed home. It was maybe a week's stay, but meeting everyone felt really good. I almost couldn't believe how much they had changed, and they couldn't believe how much I had. They wanted to know about Korea and how my time was there.

It was such a different experience that I didn't want to miss out on a single detail. Koreans are people who like to learn, and I felt like I could relate with them on that front. They always wanted a head start in learning the language – they were eager to know what certain things meant and would constantly try to implement it in their language. For me, though, it was very difficult to understand them. They had a different way of speaking, and even though I was trying to learn their language, it was still difficult to follow.

But now that I was home, all I could think about was my trip to Germany. I really didn't want to leave, but that fated day arrived sooner than I thought. Once again, I was packing up, saying goodbye and heading out to a whole new world. It felt like that goodbye was getting heavier with each time.

I kept looking out at the passing clouds throughout the flight and wondered how my new life would be. A glumness and excitement filled me with every passing cloud beneath us. Finally, as soon as we touched down, I could feel the difference in the air. We landed in Frankfurt, Germany, and the air was sort of cold. I found out that I would be stationed in Giessen at the HHB 42nd Field Artillery Brigade.

Coach Dr. Wilson in Germany at 19 years old

I was immediately taken to the headquarters, where I was assigned my work. As it turned out, my job there would be as a specialist at the Motorpool. If I'm being honest, it was frustrating because I didn't get promoted in Korea as I thought I would be. I wanted to be a Sergeant, but that simply was not happening. The problem was that once you got the E-4 ranking, it was difficult to jump over to Sergeant. If I really wanted it, I would have to put in a lot of effort – more than what I had put in till now.

Regardless, the more I thought about it, the more I figured it could be done. I was already airborne, so I couldn't let it discourage me that so many people had already moved ahead.

I had to give in the time, and while it did take some time to get the discharge and the rank, I was willing to do whatever it took.

Back in Korea, my job required me to go out and be in the fields for weeks at a time. We had to have discipline and patience. We didn't have any natural light out there; all we had was infrared light. If there was anything we had to do, it was done under discipline. We had to be on guard duty at night and put up G.P. large tents for the soldiers to sleep in.

Apparently, I knew how to do it properly, which was why everybody would often come up to me for that. It was quite difficult in the field; we would make back and forth runs from the company, then back to the field, and then stay there for the week.

The field would become our home – we had to do everything there. We had to eat, sleep, go to the bathroom, and accept the fields as our new home. It was the first experience I had in Giesen, and while it was a difficult time there, we could easily take the train and go to Frankfurt.

Frankfurt always seemed like a whole new world – it felt different just being there. We didn't have to worry about the constant runs, and we had food just like at home. Burger King, McDonald's, and all the different restaurants we found back in the States. It was like a little piece of home – one that I was so desperately deprived of in Korea. I wouldn't say the food was exactly the same, but it was close. I could always enjoy the aroma and be granted a little nostalgia.

What I liked most, though, was the peace. The somewhat piece of silence was what I craved so desperately. When I was in the 42nd Brigade, my ears would grow accustomed to the constant noise and the constant gunshots. The only thing that put me to sleep and woke me up was the loud boom in the

44

distance. Time didn't matter – the war didn't stop. At one point, it had devastated me. I wanted a little slice of solace, but I couldn't find it. I knew my ears were being affected because every time someone would say something, I would have to strain my ears to listen to them.

We were provided earplugs for them, but when blasts go off every five minutes, it's safe to say that the plugs were completely useless. It was a constant surge of noise, and there was absolutely no way to block it out. However, it wasn't all that bad because, eventually, we would be granted our time away from the constant stress. The best thing about the unit, though, was the gym – it was absolutely beautiful.

I would be up well before sunrise and watch the clear sky. I would often stand there, reveling in the silence and watching the smoke in the distance. There was a haunting calmness that often filled the land. Once the cold would begin settling into my bones, I would head toward the gym. It was like a routine, and I would usually end up playing basketball there. That was the only thing I looked forward to the most.

Eventually, all that practice was worth it because I was able to play basketball for the company. I could always push myself, and I knew it was for my own growth. At one point, it felt like everywhere I went, I would be selected to play.

In Germany, though, I was just a starter. I would try to make the most of everything I could, and most of all, I developed an interest in collecting. I would collect albums, movies, and things like that. When in Geissen, I would go to the downtown music stores and buy the latest records they sold. However, while my collector's ability improved, I realized something else, I was also improving in my game. We ended up winning the company championship by playing against other companies.

I was working through the hardships and excelling in everything I put my mind to. One of these things was the inspections. Inspections were a crucial part of the Army. At first, the inspections were general; they would randomly come in and ensure that everything was proper, especially the dressing. I always got a 100% in it. So many great things came by during my time here; it made me proud.

Of all the things, Giessen renewed my faith in myself. It didn't just grant me opportunities, but it gave me experiences I couldn't part with. The two years I spent there was something I couldn't let go of, and it wasn't just the medals that were a constant reminder.

I took those experiences to become the man I truly am. For two years, I struggled there. I would often call home, and just listening to them would get me close to a breakdown. I missed them terribly, and I missed home.

After about two years, my time in Giessen ended, and I was gratefully making my way back home. You'd think I'd be used to life by now, and while the constant traveling did expand my experiences, I couldn't help but feel a tinge of tiredness for the nomadic lifestyle I had grown to accept.

Germany was, in all, a great experience. It helped me grow and become a better version of myself. As I sat in the plan, re-thinking my life, I couldn't help but backtrack on everything that happened. I never thought I would be able to spend a month there, and here I was, returning after two years and feeling as though everything had changed.

I was on my way to Fort Belvoir in Virginia, my new home. I would be given a new job there, and the process would start again. It was almost the same with every station – it felt like I was working my first job but still holding everything I learned in the past. Here, they stationed me in a nonosecond engineer company. It wasn't an easy job, but then again, the previous jobs weren't either.

At this point, it felt like all the companies I was stationed in required outdoor work and were very difficult to handle. This time, the company built bridges from one end to another using a boat. They were actually called floats, and I was the logistics supply sergeant in the unit. I was at a standstill at that point in my career and had faced no growth. It was undoubtedly frustrating being an E-4 for such a long time.

I thought my time in the military was up, and while it was a comforting thought, I had to push forward. Eventually, instead of leaving, I re-enlisted for about six more years.

The only thing that bothered me was that I had already decided to go home after my four years were up. However, once I finished that tour, it would be ten years, and I figured that if I could do ten years, then doing another ten and retiring wouldn't be an issue.

What made the decision easier was how Fort Belvoir was closer to home, and, this way, I could go home at least four times a week. I loved that freedom, I had needed it from the very beginning, and this time, I had it. Of course, I couldn't go home every day, but just four days was more than enough. I had my own home, which was around forty-five minutes away, so there was more leverage for me.

I had two roommates, and they were both from Alabama. They were great guys, and I bonded with them quite well. It made my time easier there. After a hard day, we would usually just hang out, sipping on a beer and talking. They had a great sense of humor; one of the guys was from Jackson, and the other was from Harlow, and what I liked about them was how open they were about everything. They would tell me how they had friends going to school at Howard University, and so it became very familiar to me.

I didn't know that that was the beginning of just another change that would enter my life.

Chapter 8

"Life is not a problem to be solved, but a reality to be experienced."

Soren Kierkegaard

When I look back at my life, I realize how much it has changed. There was a time when I couldn't study in the college I wanted due to the lack of funds, and now I had more than enough to opt for any college I wanted. It was all because of hard work and dedication.

Now that my roommates were friends with people from Howard University, I could go with them to gatherings there. How things proceeded after that very much imparted my personal life. It all happened on an incredibly slow summer night when the outside silence was seeping into the room. I was lost in my thoughts as I stared up at the white walls in my room when I heard laughter piercing through the silence. I walked outside to see my fellow soldiers and friends Barlow and Jackson flopped over the couch.

"What's up?" I asked as I made my way toward them and sat down.

"This guy here is planning to go to Washington D.C., Howard University," Barlow said, pointing to Jackson. I lifted my eyebrow when he threw up his hands.

"Not to study, man. There's this chick there," he began, and understanding overcame my expression. I sat down and listened to him talk about one of the girls there who he wanted to mess around with. A couple of days later, we were on our way there. It wasn't necessarily to meet up with this girl, but there was a party there that she was going to be at, and I didn't want to stay behind.

Of course, I did have my fair share of parties in the Army, but something felt different that day – there was something in the air. When we turned the corner, we could already hear the music. Jackson parked right outside the house amongst the other line of cars, and we got out.

When we entered, I could only see the sea of bodies swaying with the music. We made our way past everyone until Jackson found his group of friends. That's when I met her – Lisa. She stood amongst her friends sporting a black dress. I later found out that she was a cheerleader at Howard, and after Barlow introduced her, I couldn't stay away. From that day forward, we became friends. Lisa was the woman who had left me in awe the moment I laid my eyes on her. After a while, our friendship grew, and suddenly, I didn't feel so alone, even on my loneliest days. I would go to meet her practically every day until, one fateful day, I gathered the courage and asked her out. Luckily for me, she said yes!

Finally, I was in a relationship with a woman I really liked. She was from Montgomery, Alabama and worked at Church's Chicken. I played basketball for the base at Fort Belvoir, and she was the cheerleader. At the time, she was in her sophomore year, and every time I would have a game, she would always come down to watch it. On my team was a guy named Kevin, and he was from D.C. He had graduated from Dunbar high school in Washington D.C. Since he was from the same neighborhood, we became really good friends. Kevin would usually invite his girl, Crystal, to the game, and Lisa would be there. We had all managed to become great friends, and I truly believe that that bond I had with Kevin enhanced our game as a team. Through our hard work, we ended up winning the Post Basketball Championship at Fort Belvoir. It was one of the most memorable championships: the hard work, the consistent practices, everything. In the end, it all paid off.

It was just good news from there on out. Lisa and I would eventually form a serious life-changing relationship, and within the next couple of years, we ended up having a son who we named Kevin Wilbon Jr.

The entire experience was fairly overwhelming. The thought that I was finally going to be a dad had surged emotions in me that I didn't quite understand then. Lisa was pregnant with Kevin Jr. when I was stationed in Germany, and while I wanted to be there to experience everything, my job stopped me from it. Regardless, as much as I had my eyes on success, I felt like I was missing out on a significant portion of my life. And so, after a long discussion with Lisa, we decided that she was going to move here.

Germany was rough; at that time, they stationed me in one of the world's coldest places: Wildflicken Germany. It was undoubtedly beautiful, but it snowed around ten months throughout the year. Wildflicken was the home to Baroque buildings and a view you simply could not get enough of. It was just the cold that was difficult to manage, but I was finally on the way to being promoted, and I couldn't compromise on it. I had put in years of effort, and my dreams were finally coming true.

I would often think about it, the path my life was

set on, and it made me happy. I was reaching a position in life that I had always dreamed of, and only a few years ago, I couldn't even imagine it. The best part about becoming a sergeant was that you could easily move into your own place off-post.

When the ceremony took place, my mind was alive with the possibilities. It felt surreal, and the only thing I could think of at that point was the pride I felt for myself and my parents would feel for me. Now, I had the title of a Sergeant and a dad, both of which once felt as though they were out of my reach. When Lisa came over, it was difficult for her, as I had expected it to be. The snow was too much to handle, and the cold made the environment a completely different feel to it – it didn't feel like home.

Lisa tried to get used to it but, eventually, she couldn't and left for home. She had gotten a job there, and while I wanted my son with me, I couldn't actually stop her. It hurt me quite a lot. I felt as though a part of me was taken away. It was difficult enough to be in a strange land, but to have my son move away broke me.

It's safe to say that Lisa and I didn't stay together for too long. We were both young and still trying to make our place in our careers. I, too, didn't handle grief so well either; I did things I shouldn't have been doing. It had a lasting effect on both of us. I wasn't fully committed the way I should have been. One thing led to another, and I succumbed to the pressure of it all. We decided that the best way to move forward was to end the relationship. I had made peace with the fact that I would never be able to have the first moments with my son, and while that was a pain that burdened my heart, I had to deal with it.

I had a responsibility to my son, and though he was far away, I still had to take care of him. I learned along the way that I have seen people treat marriage as though it is just another rite of passage. In reality, though, I learned about the sanctity of marriage; about how it defines a whole new stage in your life. It's more than just something you have to do because it's right. That's what I learned far into the future when I grew and matured from the man I used to be.

With marriage, you have to be committed to the ups and downs and the constant changes coming by, and the only way you can do that is when you're ready. I wasn't, and I understood that later on in life. I took responsibility for my actions – it was something that the Army had shaped me to become.

I truly do believe that there's a power to maturity and understanding where you're wrong. In order to understand, you have to allow yourself to become that person. I became that person when I allowed myself to change. It was all a gradual process; nothing happened overnight.

It actually came about when Kevin junior came into my life. The fact that I was now a father meant that I had to sort out my problems and get my life in order. I had to change myself to set an example for him, and the more I thought about the man I was, the more I knew I couldn't help my son become better.

Before him, I was carefree. I cared more about my own motives than someone else. Now, though, I was responsible for a child – I had to set an example so he could learn from me and grow to become a man who would make a difference in the world. After Lisa, I spent a long time in retrospect evaluating everything in my life.

I would spend most of my nights up thinking about the example I was setting for my son. I knew I had to change my ways before it was too late. The Army had taught me enough about change, and I did owe most of it to my experiences. However, the realization is all it takes to implement it. The sense of accountability finally put my priorities in perspective. It had a big impact on my life, and I felt as though it changed everyone around me too.

All it takes is one person to change; once they do, everyone else follows suit. I saw that – when I began putting in the effort for change, others moved accordingly. It was anything but easy, and I wasn't prepared for it. Being a dad was more than just about taking care of the basic needs. It was now about him and I together, as one. My way forward in my career was dependent on how it would impact him.

That was where I became certain about my decision in the military. I was going to have to do twenty years, so my son received everything that I was deprived of. I wanted to lay out all the possibilities in front of him and teach him how giving up was never the answer, no matter how difficult situations became. I thought of my lifestyle when I was younger and how we tried our best to make ends meet. I knew my son wouldn't have to deal with that problem.

I would often talk to the younger soldiers about my journey, telling them about my situation. I would discuss how I became a sergeant and how they could as well. My son showed me that I wasn't just a position in my career; I was responsible for the change around me. That's how I began. I viewed the soldiers I was in charge of from a completely different light. Now, they weren't just soldiers; they were men who would bring a change to this world.

I flipped the switch, and I was now in charge of growing people. It wasn't easy because being a sergeant meant that I was in the field a lot, and eventually, I moved back to the motor pool because they needed someone with my experience. I was happy with it; at least I wasn't a supplier anymore. I had more responsibility that came with the job title.

It was a lot of moving around, though. I had a variety of different things to do, and I would go around Germany to do it. I would pick up different supplies, drop them off. There was fuel, vehicles, transportation, booking, and there were times when I wished I hadn't actually gotten the position. That was, of course, once the initial excitement died away. However, the regret didn't come close to how much I appreciated it. I was ready to take on the challenges. It was mainly all that driving. I eventually even received an award for it – as it turned out, I had driven a specific number of miles, roughly around 250,000 in Germany alone. I had easily become an expert driver. It was amongst the several other rewards I had received over the years. There was something that I was preparing myself for, though. I knew that the moment I left Germany and returned to the states, I would have to become a full-time dad. And all the experiences I learned here wouldn't still not be enough for that.

It was a whole new chapter I was ready to take on.

Once I returned to the states, I got stationed at the Walter Army Medical Center in Washington D.C. It was a beautiful but small base, but the best thing about it was I was back at home! It felt as though a lifetime had passed, and I feel that familiar sense of freedom you felt at home.

The entire journey took me places – beautiful places – but nothing compared to home. After all, I was born and raised in Washington D.C. and being in the Army working there was a dream come true. However, there were a lot of things that were await for me, and I was soon to find out.

Walter Reed was a challenge because I was thrown into a top leadership position at the Headquarters Medical Center Brigade as the NCOIC of the entire Brigade as Sergeant E-5 put into a Sergeant First Class E7 position. I took on several jobs at the Medical Center Brigade, getting certified in various positions, attending the top NCO schools because of my position. Nevertheless, I was back in the nation's capitol, where I actually had to get away from as a youngster because of the bad surroundings of crime and murder. Would I fall back into that type of life because I was back home? The answer was no way because I grew into becoming a responsible man and father and knew the value of life and hard work, not to mention being a father. These things were the most important things in the world to me. Being in charge of a lot of soldiers and trying to run a supply room at the same time was definitely challenging because I had to be responsible for grown people, married and single, dealing with their problems and supervising them at work as well, but I was up for the challenge.

In fact, I did so well as the NCOIC of Brigade Supply that our supply room never failed a company or supply room inspection, and I received numerous awards and accolades for my achievements. This is thanks in part to my counter partner who helped me run the supply room; his name is Darrell Campbell, a soldier from Fayetteville, N.C. He was a very knowledgeable soldier in the field of logistics, and he kept the medical center brigade supply room running smoothly. Walter Reed was a struggle because of all of the personal struggles that I was dealing with. Since I was at a medical facility, I decided to attend EMT (Emergency Medical Technician) school, which was six months and required a lot of my time and studying. I ended up graduating as a certified EMT and put that feather in my cap. In any event, I made sure that I was a great father to Kevin Jr.

Coach Dr. Wilbon & Son Kevin Jr

I spent every second that I could with him when I wasn't working. Being a father is a 24-hour job and must be taken seriously because you no longer have the luxury of just trying to take care of yourself. You have another life you are responsible for, and I took that very seriously.

Chapter 9

It takes courage to grow up and become who you really are.

E.E. Cummings

If there's anything I learned about adulthood, it's the fact that it's unpredictable, and there's strength in unpredictability. When I heard about my son being taken home, that was yet another thing I had to learn how to deal with. Little did I know that there was a lot more ahead. I still had about ten years remaining. All I knew now was that I was back home to the familiar city scents and the people I had left behind.

I was stationed at the Walter Reed Army Medical Center, and I was in charge of the Medical Center Brigade. Under me were around 30 soldiers, and I had to take care of all the companies in that post. It wasn't as easy as it sounds; there were about fifteen to twenty companies with over 1500-3000 soldiers.

Essentially, it was meant to be a Sergeant First Class E7 slot, but since I was the only Sergeant there, I was put in charge. I was working in the position of someone who would outrank me by two ranks, and, of course, that was just a lot of extra work. I didn't mind it since it served as an opportunity for me to learn. I was required to handle all the logistics supplies of the soldiers and manage the financing and ledgers of the logistics. It was pretty much worth the challenge since that made me legible for the Army Achievement Medals and Army Accommodation Medals, which I received along with them a couple of Meritorious Service Medals – the highest medal you could receive in the Army at peacetime. I was over the moon with excitement. Life was finally on track, not to mention that I had also met this gorgeous woman I instantly hit a connection with. I had met her at just the right time in my career, and she worked in housing at Walter Reed. That was where I had to send married soldiers to get places to stay for their families. She was a beautiful woman who had caught my attention the moment I laid eyes on her. Her name was Chris, and she was also from the D.C. area, born and raised. She was very feisty and loud and didn't take any mess from anyone, no matter what rank. That was the thing that attracted me to her.

Coach Dr. Kevin Wilson Sr. and his beautiful wife Chris A. Wilson

Chris was the woman who had all the soldiers try to ask her out, and while I often did her about how gorgeous she was, I never actually got to meet her. I knew a lot of soldiers who she had turned down.

I got my chance to meet her on a relatively calm Monday afternoon when I went over to housing to get information on an apartment for me. As luck would have it, she was there. She helped me find a nice place in Virginia, and that was the start of our relationship.

Our relationship only grew, and I knew I was falling in love with her as time went on. When things started to get serious, she invited me to meet her mom. Boy, oh boy, was I nervous! I remember not being able to sleep the entire night before the meet while Chris tried to calm me down. I had faced a lot of difficult situations, but this one was something I wasn't prepared for.

However, when the day came, it all went very smoothly. I can remember this day for the rest of my life because her mom was straightforward and candid with me and expressed that if my intentions with Chris weren't positive, I needed to leave her alone.

Successfully, I got approval from her mom and her sister Cheryl, who was pretty like her sister. I could finally breathe! Her family was very welcoming of me and our relationship. Eventually, I introduced them to my son Kevin Jr. and they thought he was cute and said that he looked just like me. After moving into my apartment, I got several part-time jobs to supplement my income because living in Virginia was expensive. I worked at J.C.

Pennys and Athlete's Foot Sports Store to help pay my bills. The meaning of responsibility and accountability as a man and a father to me spared me any shame in taking on part-time jobs to support my means of living because in life, I feel that you do what you have to do to support yourself and your family, this was a lesson that was taught to me by my family. I can recall one day after I got back from Germany, I went to visit my grandfather in the rough neighborhood of D.C. I was driving my brand new Saab 900S that I purchased from Germany a local drug dealer who I grew up with and went to school with had his drug-dealing friends stop my car in the middle of the street.

They asked me what was my business in the area, and once my old friend recognized me, he came over to the car and gave me a handshake and started talking to me. He asked how I was doing, especially being in the military, and I told him great. He told me that the car was driving was ok but nothing compared to the cars and trucks he had lined up on that entire street; he went on to tell me that if I came to work for him that he could get me ten of the cars that I was driving, I told him no thanks and that I'm doing fine doing what I'm doing.

He laughed at me and told me to enjoy living the low life and told his dealers to let me by, and I proceeded to leave the area. I'm saying that I'd rather work hard for what I've got than do the wrong things to get fast money and risk the chance of going to jail or dying. After that conversation with my old friend, I really knew that I've outgrown the streets and the mentality of fast money and trying to get over on people for my gratification and personal gain. I thought about the rough and tough neighborhoods I used to hang out at, like Suewam Cords, Barry Farms, Ivy City, Trinidad Ave, Chillum Road, Hillcrest Heights, Peppermill Village, Georgia Ave in Northwest DC and Kenilworth Ave, to name a few. These places are important to mention because I learned the real meaning of boosting and learning street life. I thought about my cousin Jose Brooks who gave me wisdom and knowledge about how to survive the streets. I thought about my cousins and the White family I frequently visited.

I also thought about how, sometimes, I would have to fight at parties because of the area that we were in, over on 50th place N, E. These were some of the things that I talk about to people who are going through trials and tribulations in their lives. I am a father, and co-parenting Kevin Jr. was difficult, of course, to top all the happenings in my life at that point, but it wasn't something I minded. However, things took a turn for the worst when I visited my parents. While I was getting used to the good news filing up my life, there was darkness making its way into the family – it was at that time mom was diagnosed with breast cancer.

She had actually been struggling for years and had battled the illness as hard as she could, but when I returned from Germany, she was at the final stage. She was a woman with so much strength that I couldn't even imagine it. The illness had taken her will, but it never took away the spark in her eyes. My mom has been my best friend, my confidant, and my rock throughout all my years. I was so used to seeing her always out and about that when I met her then, I refused to accept that mom had fallen so. I don't know what I would do without her by my side, but I had to try and be strong for her. My heart broke every time I would hold her frail hands, and I had decided then that I would spend every minute I had with her. Cancer had spread rapidly and was slowly consuming her entire body. It had taken away her eyesight, and when I brought my son to meet her, all she could do was touch him to know who he was.

COACH DR. KEVIN WILSON SR.

It was an ache that I had to carry with me all the time – every time I went to work, I had to bury my depression and focus on my work. It was a challenge and the first challenge that I hoped so desperately to turn away. I wanted to heal her, but I knew even thinking it would cause nothing but pain. And so I held my head high while my heart sunk lower within my chest, I would go home every day to watch my mother fade away just a little bit more, her pain hurting me instead. I turned to God then for help, the one thing my mother instilled in me, and He did.

Eventually, after eight long months of struggle, my mother left us all, leaving me with a gaping emptiness within.

Mum was the woman who gave me life, taught me right from wrong, and gave me advice and strength to be the man I was. Without her, I felt lost. Nothing made sense, and I tried my best to apply her words to my life. I tried my best to keep myself occupied, and it helped. However, I would still see her in everything I did. I heard her constantly telling me that God has a plan and I shouldn't question it.

"Put your trust in Him, and He will guide you through," she would always say. That's exactly what I did. I trusted God and believed in Him. However, this particular part of life was tough – it was difficult to accept it.

Now, I had to focus on my career and my family the best I could. They needed me, and I wasn't doing any good by dwelling on my mother's death. I knew that's not what she would have wanted either. So, one day, I got up, forced myself out of bed, and vowed to get my life together again.

As time went on, life became a little better. The darkness that had taken over me was slowly dissipating, and I moved on to putting my energy into raising my son.

He was a little older now, and I had the opportunity to raise him the way I thought was best. Then, I decided I was going to put him into sports. I began to coach him in basketball, football, and baseball. Things were finally falling into place, my relationship with Chris grew, and we were beginning to see each other regularly. Chris was the woman who gave me strength and showed me that everything was going to get better.

I noticed a change in Kevin Jr. as well. He has really begun to blossom into the boy I had envisioned him to be. He excelled in all the sports he played, and the more I coached him, the more I realized that others would stand watch. Everyone was impressed by the kid, from family to the soldiers and their families. I wouldn't say it was easy; taking care of Kevin Jr. was more than just coaching him.

I was aware of my responsibility, and I realized that taking care of only myself was a luxury. I had to pay attention to the sacrifices and effort I had to put in. It's something parents need to understand as well. Taking care of yourself is a luxury. However, having another life holding on to you and keeping you accountable for your actions is a whole different story.

I thought about my own parents and how they took care of my siblings and me. They understood us and tried to mold us into how the world worked. My brothers and I applied that to our life the best we could, and I knew that my son would do the same. All I had to do was give him time.

I've seen most parents making that mistake – instead of giving their time, parents tend to shower their kids with money or material things. That's a great distraction, of course. But, eventually, the kid grows up to prioritize other things. Your concepts will not run well with them, mainly due to the lack of attention or love when they were little.

That's what I did with Kevin Jr. I was there for him; I guided him, taught him everything I knew, and shaped him to be ready for the world.

However, in order to do that, you also have to understand your kid. Every child is different and requires a different set of skills. What may work with my kid might not necessarily work with yours. However, the bottom line is always the same – kids love attention, and all they really look for is their parents giving that to them. They need to know that you're there and will do everything in your power to protect and guide them.

I didn't really have much time on my hands, but what little I did, I spent with K.J. I made sure I would take time out to take care of him and take him with me wherever I could. It wasn't just the financial aspect of taking care of him, but the mental and physical aspect of it too.

And making sure that he knew that just because I wasn't with his mom, I still loved him and, you know, things that wasn't going to change as far as me being there for him. So that's, I think that's a very important thing is in order to, you know, to be a good parent, you have to give your time. You have to give your love, and you have to make sure no matter what's going on in your life, you know, whether you're working hard, you got a whole lot of different things going on personally in your life, that you set aside time for your kids.

My coaching helped him prosper. I coached up at Ft. Meade, an army base in Maryland. I was moving myself up, and I wasn't just coaching my son but also other kids. Now, I would mentor the kids, sharing my experiences and teaching them what I learned from it all. There was something exciting that gathered the kids around a veteran, and they listened just as intently as I told it.

My experiences were setting up their goals, and they tried to learn the most they could from what I had to offer. We were all a team trying our best to make things work. Eventually, we ended up winning numerous of Championships in all three sports. My coaching was a huge success, and I coached all ages, from eight to eighteen girls and boys.

I hadn't given up on the military, though. I was flourishing there as well and ended up getting promoted to Staff Sergeant. It was something I had been looking forward to for so long and having it finally happen felt amazing. I couldn't help but think of mom and how proud she would be of me. I was in the position I wanted to be in, and I was up for a desperately needed pay raise!

Everything was going right until reality came knocking on my door once again. I received the orders to be stationed at Ft. Hood, Texas, with my headquarters being at Ft. Sam Houston in San Antonio, Texas. I wasn't happy with this, and I knew it would damper my relationship with my son and Chris. However, this was the military, and I had no say in it. I made my way to my loves with a heavy heart, my heart breaking with every step I took. I could only hope that Chris would understand. K.J. was going to be tougher to handle, but I had to do my best.

I had been stationed in a lot of places a lot of times, but this was the most difficult thing I had to face. I couldn't imagine what would happen, but I gathered my courage and vowed to myself to keep our relationship going no matter the distance. Chris was very understanding and supported me. I don't think I would have the courage if it weren't for her. I held her memory close to give me strength every day as I left.

The days went by quickly, and before I knew it, it was time for me to leave. There I went again, being away from my son. It was a pain I couldn't quite place, but I had to work out a plan with his mother for visitation, especially since I would be in another state days away. A new chapter was beginning.

**

Texas was just another long list of traveling that I was doing with my unit. Once again, I was back to the routine of going from one place to another – I went to the Midwest to assist and train army reserve units in logistics. On the weekends, I was on the move to places like Oklahoma, Arkansas, Kansas, Seattle, California, Wyoming, and Colorado, to name a few. It certainly wasn't a piece of cake; I spent countless days and sometimes weeks there away from my own base. Life was nothing more than a large list of travels with no rest. I missed home, and I missed my son. However, I knew that all of this was for them. Chief Boone, my warrant officer in charge, took me under his wing and taught me everything I knew about dealing with the reserve and national guard units in logistics and transportation from the various states we visited. He was, quite frankly, one hell of a teacher. However, my willingness to learn also helped me go a long way. All it really takes is effort, and once you have effort, you can make things work. That effort had brought me here, and I knew that it was going to take me far. One of the best things, though, was the people. I absolutely loved how I was able to meet so many different people with so many stories to tell.

It was a unique experience meeting them from all these states, making valuable contacts and acquiring knowledge for my future references and upcoming endeavors. However, every minute there made me realize how much I was missing in my life. The thoughts of Chris and my son were all but eating me up. I knew that whenever I would have time, I would have to make arrangements for them. Right now, though, I would find whatever time I had and fly home to visit Chris and my son K.J. All the while, I also continued college, trying to pursue my degree the best I could. I was actually opting for a General Studies degree, and I was getting it from the Central Texas College while working at Walter Reed. It was a whole lot of work with no rest. I was taking night courses which meant that my entire days and nights were occupied by work. I had no time for myself, and this busyness helped keeping me from dwelling too much on my loss.

I would get out of work once every two or three weeks, and that was all I had to take care of myself and my family. I was familiar with Central Texas College because Chris used to go there too. She had also gotten her associate's degree from there and helped me with everything I needed help with. We would actually go there together if it weren't for the days.

I continued on going to college to time permitted me to pursue my degrees because knowledge is power. I knew that was something I couldn't leave behind. It really didn't matter how much I was excelling in my career, what mattered was the education. At the end of the day, I knew I had some and it was coming in place of my growth. There was more good news ahead though.

It wasn't long after being in Texas, and I had received great news that Chris was pregnant with my child. I was out of my mind with excitement.

The fact that I was going to be a father once again had consumed all my thoughts. I was ready, and after K.J., I was prepared for whatever was going to come forth. Now came when I also had to look at my financial standing. Could I provide the same lifestyle to my new child as I could with K.J.? I now had one more mouth to feed, so I had to look for more options.

After finding out the news, I knew that I had to get another part-time job so that I can help put Chris into a home. She needed all the care and attention since she was pregnant with my baby. Life was almost on track save for the fact that I wasn't home. I had to make time, and that's what I did. I flew back home and drove back as much as I could, which wasn't much because of my demanding job and schedule. I had to make as much time as possible, and even that didn't seem enough. I knew my priorities, though, and my priority was Chris and my kids. I loved her with all my heart, and she had brought meaning to my life once again.

I knew what I had to do, and after a lot of consideration, I went home to marry Chris in a small, intimate ceremony at the Justice of the Peace in Arlington, Virginia. It was beautiful, and Chris managed to capture my heart once again when she came in front of me adorned in a white dress. K.J. was right next to her, holding her dress.

Chris' beautiful mother, Josesina Maxen, was there with her precious grandmother Maggie Washington. Her beautiful aunt, Yvonne Gowdy, and wonderful sister, Cheryl, witnessed the joining of our hands in matrimony. However, unlike other events, I couldn't stay back long. Right after that, I had to get back to Ft. Hood in a hurry. It wasn't easy; I became an armed security officer that moonlighted the clubs in Temple, Austin and Killeen, Texas. I worked all day and all night at least four times a week to help support my woman.

The only problem now was my Sergeant. In spite of everything that was going on, I was having a rough time in my unit with my first sergeant, we didn't see eye to eye on a lot of things, and he was making it hard for me to get promoted to the next grade. I felt as though he was purposely holding me back, like a personal grudge he wasn't willing to let go. It had reached the point that he wouldn't even let me take leave to see my baby being born.

That was one of the things I simply couldn't let go of. Chris ended up having my son Kevon without me being there, and I was upset that I wasn't present for his birth. It broke my heart that I was stuck in a situation I didn't want to be in. Chris was having issues back home and needed me there.

I ended up going to the National Louis University. And I got my Bachelor's degree in business management in Texas. During this time, I was again in charge of a battalion. I was a battalion logistics NCO, which required a lot of traveling all over the Midwest. Once again, my routine became hectic.

I trained people, got to know them, and trained people in the reserves. We would do go to different states like Oklahoma, Kansas, Arkansas, California, Washington, and Wyoming, to name a few. I actually spent three years there. And while I was there, I was taking care of my wife in Washington, DC.

I knew that I had to make amends for my absence, and the more I thought about it, the more I knew what the solution would be. We ended up getting a place for her and Kevon, and we were grateful. However, I must say that I worked hard as an armed security guard breaking up fights at clubs, sometimes having to put people out often and even drawing my weapon on a few occasions.

Coach Dr Wilbon & son Kevon

On top of that, I also had to pay for the apartment I was living in, in Texas, as well as the single-family home that we purchased for us back in Maryland. Over time and a lot of effort later, we figured out a way to get me back to D.C. before my tour was up in Texas so we could be together. I had to prepare myself for yet another round of changes coming my way. I knew that I would miss my mentor, Chief Boone. After all the struggles I went through, he was the one who taught me the lessons which helped me excel. He showed me different situations and taught me about adversity and how to persevere through it. Through him, I learned how to deal with different people and make sacrifices for the greater good.

Chief Boone was a man who held his values firm – if there's one thing he taught me, it was that there are always consequences for the actions you make. Often, when I would find myself falling into the abyss of emotional breakdown, I would have only a few words to follow. Chief Boone said them, and I would likely give up hope if it wasn't for him.

"Life is filled with tough situations, and sacrifices are part of the process," he would say.

While I found myself in the battle with sadness, these words helped me keep hope and the fact that I had another mouth to feed. I wouldn't let my family look up to a man who ran away from things when they began to get tough. I knew that going back home to be stationed in the DMV was going to be tough, especially since I was a dad for the second time and my responsibilities were now twice the duty. However, on the brighter side to that was that I would have my sweetheart, Chris, there to help me.

Chris was and always is, my rock. Without her support, I don't think I would be able to do half the things I did. The best part of it is that my status in the military didn't make a difference to her. All she needed was that I was there for her and I gave her the love she deserved and that's what I did. In return, she gave me a family and all the happiness I have in my life. It didn't matter how difficult our life got, she was there. Throughout the time I was stationed in Texas, I missed her terribly, and she missed me too. There was an emptiness without her and I knew I had to go back. There wasn't anything we wouldn't do for each other. Soon though, the Army ended up stationing me at Ft. Myer which is in Virginia, not too far from D.C. That was great because I was closer to home. I could have visited anytime because I was stationed at Fort Myers in Virginia.

Coach Dr. Kevin Wilson Sr. SSG Wilson in the US Army

Over there, I ended up in the Headquarters Garrison Unit as the Logistics NCOIC and also worked at the Central Issuing Facility (CIF) as the NCOIC. This distributed clothing, equipment, and tools to all the soldiers on that post. Both jobs were demanding and I worked numerous hours to keep everything in tip-top shape. In all the years I have been working, I think that was the most difficult time of my life. Right now, I don't just have the responsibility of work but also my family.

Staying away from them was more difficult than I could imagine. Since I was now a father to two boys, I also knew that I had to step up my game a little more. I took fatherhood very seriously and there wasn't anything I wouldn't do for my boys. There was only one thing in my mind; I wanted to set an example for them so that they would see that hard work is a must and you must be in a strong frame of mind to take on the responsibility of other people's lives as well as your own.

COACH DR. KEVIN WILSON SR

I would often think back on my life, often thinking about how it used to be. I used to think back on my parents' values that helped me reach where I am now and the perseverance that pushed me to get out of the life we used to lead. Now, I had to put that same perseverance in my kids. While I had focused on getting my degree as well, I made sure my kids remained on the top of my priority.

Getting my associate's degree was yet another achievement, but it wasn't enough. So I went back to school to finish up yet another degree and add it to my repertoire. This time, it was my Bachelor's degree in Management. I mainly wanted to expand my horizon and have a backup plan for when I got out of the military. I didn't want to be one of those guys who had no idea what they would do after leaving the military. I had kids who were looking up to me and if I gave up now, I wouldn't be able to set an example for them. After completing my Bachelor's Degree at National-Louis University I embarked on taking it to the next level which was my Master's Degree (MBA). I studied my MBA at Toro University in California, but they had a satellite office in Virginia.

I also started coaching my son, K.J., again. It was amazing because I got to watch him grow and slowly get better in sports. That was the start of something different. I decided that since I was coaching K.J., then what was stopping me from coaching other kids? It was a great opportunity that I wouldn't want anyone to miss out on.

I thought about it. Time was a concern but not so much that I would completely stop pursuing what I had in mind. I made time and branched out to start coaching older kids on the base in basketball. I was completely certain that this would go just the way I wanted and I was right. All my years in the military prepared me for this day and I couldn't be more grateful. I applied the tactics I had learned, making sure I divided my attention equally amongst all my kids.

After all, these were all kids. After a month or so, I noticed that I did quite well. They were all happy and they enjoyed themselves. The fact that they took it as a sport rather than a competition allowed them to do well. Eventually, a coach from the neighboring high school took notice of my coaching skills. Coach Gerald Moore Jr. was from Arundel High School and was well known for his game. He watched me every time the kids would gather around, and the improvement in their games caught his attention. "He introduced himself to me after a basketball game asked me would you like to start coaching with me?" He approached me out of the blue.

I looked at the kids he had and I couldn't help myself. I wanted to accept the offer because I saw the potential they had but, at the same time, I knew I couldn't. To coach them, I needed extra time, which I didn't have. Regardless of how much I believed in them, there was just too much on my plate at this time and that is what I told him.

"I'm sorry, I don't have enough extra time for it," I told the coach honestly. Luckily enough, he understood but said that he would keep me in mind for future reference. Honestly, I was a little disappointed for turning down the offer.

I had grown to like coaching and it was something I could see myself doing. However, little did I know that we would connect again in a big way and make history later on. Life is surprising that way and it's something I tell everyone. The trick is to understand where your path is taking you and own it.

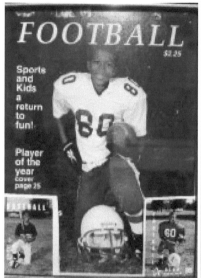
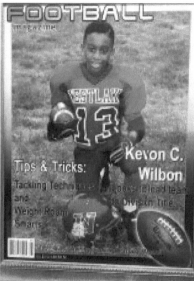

Kevon & Kevin Jr. Football pictures at 8 years old

My wife and I were making things work somehow. It wasn't easy but it was something. During that time, Chris would come along to some of my evening practices and bring Kevon along. Kevon and K.J. had, more or less, the same temperament. They both had a willingness to learn and, whenever I would play or coach the kids, there wouldn't be a moment that they would miss.

They loved imitating what I was doing, as kids often do, but that was an eye-opener for me. I always knew they would pick up what I did, but I realized how real it was when it happened in front of me. I was no longer my own person; whoever I was and whatever I did was for these kids. Chris was an athlete in her own right. She was a stunner and she had all the right moves to win a good game. She went around, winning awards, playing basketball, flag football and was an excellent tennis player as well. Her family told me about the of the grace she held when she played. It didn't matter what she was playing, she did it so passionately that, even if you weren't interested in the game, you would still not peel away from it. By now, coach Gerald had an impact on me. It didn't matter what I was doing, I would always think back at his offer. I started looking into coaching basketball in Virginia because I was working there.

Chris, on the other hand, was working at the Pentagon. After a lot of searching, I ended up coaching at several recreation centers in the city of Alexandria, Va. The kids I got throughout that time were nothing short of amazing. All of them had a vision and all they were looking for was the right push. I was there to give them that push. I learned each story, catered to every problem, and tried my best to build up everyone's morale. It was amazing, really, because I ended up winning numerous Alexandria City Wide boys and girls basketball championships.

Coach Dr Wilson & Alexandria Virginia City Wide Girls 14-Year-old East All-Stars

I wasn't doing this alone, Chris was with me throughout as well. Together, we coached the seventeen and underaged boys team at the Patrick Henry Recreation Center and there was a certain story I like to tell that happened there. I got thrown out of a game on a double technical.

However, it was Chris who took over for me and had a problem with one of the players on our team. She sure did set him straight. After finding out about the incident that occurred, I talked with the young man. I told him that if I ever hear of him disrespecting my wife, let alone a female, he would be in big trouble. I set him down and gave him the synopsis about respect in which he said that no one has ever done to him, which he appreciated. He ended up becoming a model young man and athlete. It just goes to show that, sometimes it takes a talk in a respectful way to young people to earn their respect. I picked that up along the way of my journey through the streets and life. On top Chris also helped me coach a girls basketball team who were fourteen and under at the Charles Houston Recreation in Alexandria Virginia. It was amazing to see the progress. We were all getting better ever so slowly and it was amazing. I loved watching my kids go from average players to championship winners. Our girls won the citywide championship.

In winning these basketball championships gave me great publicity because my name was getting around, and people started wanting me to coach their teams, recreation, bases, counties AAU, and High Schools were all after me. I couldn't believe that I would reach the position that I had right now. This was an exciting time in my life because I wasn't playing basketball, but I was still involved with it.

I was also doing what I loved doing – helping kids. I watched kids get better with time and opened up opportunities for themselves. Ever so slowly, I was doing my best to create a brighter future for these kids, and it was certainly helping them reach their maximum potential to make it to the next level, be it recreation, county, AAU or high school basketball teams.

It wasn't long after that we moved to Fort Washington, Maryland. That was where we were raising Kevin since we knew that it would open up better opportunities for him. On the plus side, I was also able to go over on the weekends and pick up K.J. to spend time with us. K.J. was in Columbia, Maryland with his mother but he loved spending time with his brother. He would wait for the weekends for me to come up to Columbia to pick him up. He would always be so excited to see me.

Kevon Wilson 12th Grade Prom Picture

He was a sensible kid, always learning from his observations. I was in the Military Police Company as an armorer at that time. I was also the NBC NCO – Nuclear, Biological, Chemical warfare NCO. It was a difficult job, no doubt. I was in charge of that and I would take care of the arms room. My job was to make sure that I knew every weapon, ammunition, and everything else in the artillery that the Military Police needed.

All the weapons that the military police had would be accounted for through me, but my passion for growth kept me on my toes. After I completed my MBA, I knew that I wasn't going to stop here. The military was paying for my education, after all, and it was an opportunity I couldn't let it go to waste.

I looked up courses on what I could be doing. After a lot of research, I found it – I was going to do my Master's in education. I chose this field because I figured that, since I was in the military and I was doing a whole lot of classes for the soldiers, this would only help me teach them better. It was going to shape up my time in the military and that's what I wanted to do. I wouldn't be wasting any time either. But as time went on, it was winding down. Ever so slowly, I could feel my time in the military come to an end. It wasn't in the air, but it was imminent. I couldn't stop it. I would be retired after 20 years of service but again as it always had, another letdown that would rock my world was about to happen.

Eventually, the war broke out in Iraq. At that time, I thought about the time that I served in Saudi Arabia, Desert Storm back in 1990. I was praying that I would not be getting deployed for that duty. In Desert Storm, it was tough, and nothing compared to the kinds of things I got to experience there, seeing things that I saw and doing things that I really didn't want to do that I get misty-eyed talking about, but I am a soldier and I did what I had to do to survive. When in Saudi I was holding nothing but the memories of my family close to me. I was stationed there for thirteen months it was the toughest time in my life. Getting back to me being at Ft. Myers

I was supposed to retire at that time, but when 911 took place, they actually extended my military time by four years. That was mainly because most of the soldiers are stationed abroad. That way, instead of retiring in 2001 as I was supposed to, I retired in 2005. That counted as my 24 year tenure in the military and it was one hell of a ride. I wouldn't say that it was easy but it sure did open my eyes to a whole different life that I could lead. There was still more in store for me, and that's what I had the opportunity for now. I finally retired from the military with numerous awards, achievements, experience and a wealth of knowledge that no one could put a price on. As time passed, I wasn't going to stop yet. Life is too short to put a stop to your dreams. I had only just begun my education.

I ended up teaching at the Charles County School Board in Waldorf Maryland. It was a whole new experience, and working outside of the military certainly did need some getting used to. However, I was flexible and I made it work. I taught the multicultural diversity course. Every teacher in Charles County had to come through that course before they could actually go to teach in their respective schools. In my case, I was in charge of it for around two years before moving forward. I then ended up a full-time substitute teacher teaching English at North point High School which was in Waldorf Maryland. I had also become an assistant coach to the first basketball team that they ever had that won every game its first season which was a milestone for the county in years.

Coach Dr. Wilson Northpoint High School first ever Basketball Team

Head Coach Dr. Wilson with All-Star Basketball team from the
ScoutFocus Basketball Camp Organization

Many years later, I went on to get my doctorate from North Central University. It was actually a doctorate in Education with a minor in educational leadership. Amazingly, I got a 4.0 GPA, and because of that, I got inducted into six prestigious honor societies.

Chapter 10

The key is not the will to win. Everybody has that. It is the will to prepare to win that is important.

Bobby Knight

I believe that in everything I had experienced over the years, my life only got better. From my childhood to my time in the military to the man I later became. However, it all came down to coaching. After all, it was this that brought the kick start to my real career. Coaching the kids was great exposure to a life I could lead, but the problem was that it didn't pay the bills. Regardless of how much Chris and I excelled in it, it still made us lack on the job front.

The problem was that I still had to pay my ex for KJ's child support. I had to look after him too. I tried my best to make ends meet. However, things were only getting more and more difficult by the day. I remembered my time in the military and how I had my life shaped me. I certainly was glad that my time in the military had ended but there were things we had to figure out.

Now coaching was anything but easy. From what I had seen, there were a lot of things that I still had to learn. One of those things was the fact that no amount of knowledge was ever enough, especially when it came to experiences. While the military did teach me how to instruct and lead soldiers, kids were a completely different story – especially kids from diverse background. I began fresh, re-evaluating my course of action. Kids in high school were quite a lot. They were easily intimidated and yet, had their own sense of pride. A few stood against the crowd, of course, but that was on pure luck.

Another thing I noticed was the impact of their background. Most of the time, the young men in high school came from the urban neighborhoods. In the street, they were very hard to talk to. They were bound by the things they had learned over the years. They weren't level-headed and would often not care about what you were trying to teach them. Their pride made way for excuses, which often turned into disrespect.

However, I had more than my fair share of pleasant experiences in most cases. I came across all types of kids, and went according to their eagerness to learn. However, the challenge was when the young men turned thirteen or fourteen. That was the prime age when they believed that they knew more than grownups. Their ability to listen to what was being taught significantly hindered their progress and I had to make my way around finding a middle ground.

When kids looked at me, they only saw an army man – a grownup who spent enough time in the army but not enough time playing basketball. That's where they were wrong. I couldn't blame them either; I knew so many coaches who couldn't play basketball or those who did and couldn't coach properly. Whenever I would compare myself, I believed that I had a lot to offer. I was significantly better. I was a mentor, and I had done that a lot over the years. The only thing was that I had to find a way to connect to the kids. P

The time that I coached now was a team was varsity boys between fifteen to sixteen, and some even passed for eighteen. Now, this age came with their own problems. The kids didn't just come to the game with minor problems; they dealt with real problems – things going on at home or school or a problem with their future. With them, you couldn't pinpoint the problem, but you had to empathize. Sometimes, their game was the only hope they had for making their future.

The worst part of it all was that you didn't understand your own position in their lives. If they were having trouble with something, they wouldn't tell you, and neither would they tell you if you were helping them or not. Coaching now was more than just helping out with the game – it was building their future. I saw potential in these kids, potential that most people missed out on and that was something I wanted to work with.

Being a military man, I knew that was my calling. I needed to save those who could be saved, and these kids were the ones I knew I could help out. I put myself in their shoes. If I had even one person aiding my future when I was growing up, I would have ended up in a very different situation – not that I lacked in anything now. But, perhaps, I wouldn't have to struggle as much as I did, or perhaps I would get the chance to spend more time with my mother. The possibilities are endless.

This time, I guess they were also teaching me more than I was teaching them. The exposure was different but it was a curve that could take me far in life. What I liked most about this was the fact that I had the opportunity to connect with my son. He was getting older and I wasn't missing out on the crucial moments of his life. That was a fear I had held onto for a long time, but living that moment, I could see that fear not turn into reality and I loved every minute of it.

My son was an athlete and I made sure to coach his teams as well. While there were a lot of teams under me, I still didn't want to decide to let his team go. If my son grew, I needed to be part of it, not there on the sidelines.

I guess that entire concept was what motivated me further to stay progressed on my certifications as well. I pursued my education, not wanted to put that big break in my life. I had spent too much time without a degree and now that I had started to gain the knowledge, I wasn't ready to stop.

But the coaching wasn't enough money for us, especially KJ. He was still living with his mom and I had to take care of him too. Now, Chris was at a government job which paid her pretty well. And together, we were trying our best to create a safe environment which is better for both our kids. Chris was a woman who pushed her boundaries every day, and watching her accept my first son was something I could never get out of my mind. Together, we were a family creating a stable environment for the kids.

KJ spent every other weekend with us, along with vacations, activities, and anything else we would all be doing together. It wasn't just about the money;

it was about creating a family. Most people that I have seen spend so much time in trying to ensure the monetary aspect of it that they tend to dismiss the importance of time and attention. The equality of all those factors creates a family. At the end of the day, your child's main focus will be the respect and attention you give them, not the money. A lot of people think that by being a parent, giving them money means that they're doing a great job. However to me, I think I would rather be in their life, be around them, watch them grow, and do things with him.

It's time that builds respect and time that teaches them to be the people who grow up to be decent, hardworking individuals making the world a better place. That's exactly what I was doing with my oldest son as well as my youngest. You never know the next step in life and I never wanted to spend my life regretting things I couldn't do with my kids.

Here's a pro-tip for the readers that I learned in the military; never take your life for granted. Regardless of the situation you're in, you're still living in a degree of privilege and only you have the ability to turn that privilege into something great for your kids. Every day that you wake up is, in itself, a privilege because you never know when you might breathe your last, or someone you love might leave you forever. It's in that moment that you will be hit hard at the true unfairness of life and the opportunities you missed, which you'll never be able to get back. I kept all of these things in my mind as I mapped my life out and it worked.

I made sure I defined myself not as the military man, but as a father as well. I would make sure my eldest son came to work with me to the MP companies. I would have him see what I was doing, learn my job, understand my responsibilities. He would get to spend time with me and see all the weapons as well, which would excite him the most. It came to the point where I couldn't understand if he was excited to see me or the weapons!

He had pride in being with his father, and he loved knowing more about me and my work. I guess I saw it all as part of the coaching but even coaching had its moments. Chris and I once had a kid in our team who was incarcerated. He was someone everyone talked about but we didn't know this kid. All we knew was that he was going to be on our team. This was yet something I had to learn because I had never dealt with kids who were locked up before. The problem was also that no one really wanted this kid on their team. We had to try and understand how to make him part of the team and have everyone accept him. I could have let him go, but I took a chance with him.

After all the hard work put in, he actually turned out to be amongst the best players on the team. His name was Jermaine, and he was the kid who had an impact on me. Now this kid was a loner, and he would take care of his younger brother. I had never met his parents but I knew what was going on with him because I was always talking to him. I made sure that he was comfortable and had us to rely on, and he knew that. For us, he may have been just another kid. But there was something about him that told us that we were more than just his coaches for him. He needed a shoulder to lean on and he found that with us.

It wasn't until, during one of our games, the police came and locked his little brother up that my view of life faltered just a little. I came from the streets and the position I was in now had little to do with destiny. I knew I had to stay away from jail, but there were so many moments when I could have landed in one. And then there was this kid, whose life had changed before it had the chance to even begin. It changed something in me. And that's where my mentoring journey began.

Chapter 11

"Opportunities don't happen. You create them."

Chris Grosser

When people talk to me about life, I never think about the general things I went through to get me where I am today. Instead, I am bound by the circumstances I see around me. More than myself, my definition revolved around other people's experiences of life and the impact it eventually had on me.

I believe in the power of observation. Eventually, it's observation itself that gets you a long way – observation and perception. There were a lot of instances in my life that I believe changed me without having anything to do with me. One of those instances was what I faced during coaching. I grew up in the streets; it was a life I came to know. I was one of these kids who now made up my own neighborhood at home – the kids who now saw me in awe. Throughout my life, I had seen my fair share of messed up kids – their backgrounds, situations, and life in general made them susceptible to facing failures.

However, regardless of how many times you've seen it happening, when a kid is picked up in front of you and taken to jail, there's always a part of you that curses the system. There's always that one part that wishes there was a better place for kids like them, a place that offered them opportunities they were missing out on. That was the ordeal I began to deal with, and in order to overcome it, I came up with an idea; I decided that I would get into a mentorship program. It only made sense, given how relatable these kids were and how coaching had shaped my career. I was like them in a lot of ways, and I changed my path. I could have become like them, and there were so many possibilities of that. However, how I ended up in the position I was now was something these kids could learn from. After all, how many people did they themselves know who achieved success through conventional methods?

Their definition of success was what had to change first, and I was opting to do just that. Through my time in the military and as a coach, I learned that your entire life was shaped by your mentees/subordinates' trust. If they related to you, it was easier for them to seek comfort in what you were trying to teach them—my ability to understand each child's ability and need made me a good candidate for mentorship.

Over the years, everything I had seen haunted me – I had seen violence, death, people getting locked up, and so much more. I always wondered if there was a way out – a way to make it all better – and now that there was, I wouldn't like to sit around and let the opportunity slide.

Every now and then, I would think about Jermaine's brother. I had the kid stuck in my mind for a long time after it had happened. The event was clear in my mind – we were at a basketball game when, suddenly, the cops came in looking for Jermaine's brother. I was coaching the team at this time which made matters worse. I made my players stay in place and then tried to walk up to the officer and talk to him but he wasn't ready to listen. The rest of the cops eyed each kid on the team until they landed on Jermaine's brother. I hated that sight; their view of these kids was evident. They looked at each child there – young or old – as a criminal. When they looked at Jermaine's brother, I knew immediately why they were there. While I tried my best to stop them, I had no authority there and I knew it too. I watched helplessly and in shock as the cops walked into the gym while the kid tried to run. It wasn't a pleasant sight and my breath was caught in my throat the entire time. Eventually, I watched them catch him, take out their handcuffs, and put them on the kid.

In front of everyone, they escorted him out towards their car and took him away. It was a signature move of police brutality and their lack of ability to handle situations. It was an upsetting sight, and I felt helplessness like I've never felt before. However, it was a sight that was now etched in my mind and helped me make up my mind. I was going to start mentoring at-risk youth; I knew it was going to be a lot of hard work. I was aiming at creating a structure for kids who had lost all hope for the future. I wanted to help kids who weren't just having problems at home, but also in schools and on the streets. I wanted to give back to the community that helped build me up.

All these kids needed was a push in the right direction and I was willing to give them that push. I began by coaching high school, but my first step was to reconnect with my friend once I moved to Ft. Washington. I set up an appointment and met up with coach Gerald Moore Jr. I had met him a long time ago when I had begun my coaching journey.

Back then, he had offered me a job as a coach with him at Arundel High School. The problem was that I was already in the military at the time and didn't have availability for coaching full time. Now that I had time on my hands and I was looking into it, I decided to contact him again.

As luck would have it, he had a job for me after all. He gave me an assistant coaching job at Friendly High School this time.

That marked the start of something new – I encountered a lot of kids then from a lot of different backgrounds. I was very careful about how I was going forward with my approach. If these kids got the slightest hint of how we were approaching them only because it was our job, then it would immediately push them away from us. I needed to be genuine, and I learned how over time.

I learned about the kinds of problems these kids were facing and it was quite eye-opening. At one point, I thought I knew the extent of what they faced, at the other, they were discussing things I had never even fathomed, silently praying that my own kids never had to face issues like these. They needed more than just mentorship, they needed our help to get better.

Eventually, we learned and grew to create after-school programs. We helped them with homework and made sure they were eligible enough to play basketball at a high school level. Some of the kids lacked motivation; they didn't realize the potential they held within them. However, we knew that they had to get their grades up to the mark before that. Our program helped kids to learn better than in school, and they were given tutoring to keep up their grades accordingly.

My main job, though, was that of coach. Being the assistant coach, I realized how much athletic abilities these kids held. I worked hard and catered to these specific points. We worked as hard as we could, and I pushed them to do better than the best. They overcame their challenges with consistent practices. Together, we ended up winning three Maryland State Championships. The boys' varsity basketball team ended up winning three Maryland state championships. Back then, this was a big deal and the kids certainly had their futures made out through it.

Coach Wilson's Team 3 Time Maryland State Boys Basketball Champions
Friendly High School

Coach Dr. Wilson: Friendly High School Boys Varsity Basketball Team 3 Time Maryland State Champions

On the third year, we won the Maryland 2A State Championship. What was better was that we had won back-to-championships, where we only lost one game in two years. The one game that we did lose was also not our fault; it was due to a rumor that was spread to the Maryland State Basketball Commissioner.

Coach Dr. Kevin Wilson Receiving Maryland State Championship plaque and the Friendly HS Basketball Team

An unknown person spread the rumor and it mentioned how we were carrying forward with illegal practices, which was not true. Eventually, we had no way to clear that rumor and were assessed a penalty with a loss on our record.

If everything had gone smoothly, I doubt that my kids would have been undefeated for two years in a row. The rumor had cost us a lot, but we did end up playing against schools in Pennsylvania, New York, New Jersey, and we ended up besting them at a tournament. We also had a basketball tournament over at Riverdale Baptist High School, where we beat the top three schools in Maryland, Virginia, New York, and Pennsylvania in the same day.

It was quite a boost for the kids. They had spent so much time believing they couldn't make something of themselves that they forgot how much potential they had. We had a pretty good basketball team, and we ended up besting all three schools. Everyone looked forward to playing against us, and they loved that we gave them a good competition. This is what the game was all about anyway – allowing your opponents to have fun while you beat them over and over again.

My kids were ecstatic; they had a renewed sense of trust within their own capabilities, and it was easily seen in the confidence they held. It was in the way they behaved, how they walked, and how they discussed one game after another. It was a refreshing sight to see.

We ended up having a lot of our kids go to division 1 basketball colleges and went on to graduate from those colleges. Most of the kids that played at Friendly got scholarships to the D1 schools in the aftermath, produced a professional basketball player and a professional football player that came out of our program. It wasn't just me who noticed it, the rest of the schools did too. All of a sudden, my students were known to be the best players. I helped coached a lot of very highly recruited athletes and I was fortunate enough to do it. Our kids got to go to several different formidable universities from the University of Florida to the University of Pittsburgh and so on. I was proud to see them all succeeding and going places. I had never imagined that my kids whom I helped coach would come to me with problems would grow up and end up at such high places. It was like a breath of fresh air and the life I envisioned my own kids having.

Over time, I was glad that I ended up coaching over a thousand kids. This wasn't just boys, but both boys and girls from ages six to eighteen.

I tried to keep myself busy and build a community where kids felt safe. My mentorship method was simple – I needed to get into the kids' mindsets and dissect who they were and how we could tackle what they wanted in life. It was something that was also helping me with my own kids. The more I talked to them, the more I was able to understand their purpose in life.

With some of the kids I was mentoring, I would try and understand what plans they had for the future. They had a driving force and it was my job to guide them to the right path. Eventually, I understood that they were very fascinated by my life choices. We all sat down together and discussed it most of the time, and they agreed they wanted to take the ASVAB Test. I was glad they were walking in my footsteps. They ended up going into the Army, Air Force or Marines. The kids on the street worked with the same approach. All they needed was someone to listen to and guide them, and I was playing that person's role. I would make it a habit to get to know the kids in my community and offer them any assistance they needed to get off the streets and go to college. This was about building a life they would be proud of and not fall into habits that would eventually harm their future.

In every aspect of my job, I made sure I focused on one thing – discipline. If you lack the discipline to follow your life purpose, you can reach nowhere in life. Respect your own choices and push through the boundaries that you have been placed in. Do it with consistency and you'll notice that change automatically. I have come across kids who felt as though their purpose in life was nothing, that their situations had led them to no future. However, the truth of the matter is that there is nothing that could keep you from reaching your goal. I've always emphasized discipline; whether it was in the military, at home, in education, coaching or life period, I believe that the only way forward is keeping that sense alive and allowing yourself to be the better version of yourself.

I truly believe the life lessons helped me progress the most. And through me, I was able to help these kids get an idea of who they were and where they had to do. Eventually, my dream became their dream and together, they were able to make it to the National Basketball Association, the Major League Baseball and the NFL.

The fact that I was coaching these kids was beyond my own comprehension. It was a one in a million shot and I was taking it to change the mindset of the kids who were the way I used to be. More than such success, I saw how they learnt accountability and responsibility, eventually leading to better people. Looking at them, I realized something that I was unaware of myself – sports wasn't the only way to gain their understanding. I could use my own examples and my own actions for every day problems to change the way the population thought. Sports was just for them, but my actions, or the actions of other adults around them, were for their own development. It was for changes that they could bring within them and the society. One by one, I could see the constructive change. I realized that it impacted how you were as well. I saw that the only way I, and other mentors like me, were able to make even the slightest bit of change was because we lived out lives positively as well. We genuinely cared for these kids and for the work. The genuineness in our attitudes made us successful with our work.

However, it didn't make it any less dangerous. Regardless of how we were changing the world, we were still putting our lives on the line while doing it. The streets hadn't changed from when I was a kid. If anything, it was much more dangerous now. You had to be careful with everything you did or said. If you were even close to the wrong group of kids or in the wrong neighborhood, you could easily end up shot.

There was no safety but I still tried my best to put away my fears and be there for them. After all, I had been in the military for so long, I had picked up a thing or two about safety measures. My approach to mentorship and coaching was simple – healthy discussions. I would often discuss my journey with the young boys and girls under my care. They would get an insight on how I used to live and the choices that I made. They learned that circumstances had the ability to change, and that people had the ability to change as well. It was eye-opening how much they were able to take in. However, while I was proud at how much these kids were changing, nothing came close to the pride I felt for my own sons. They, too, had begun to walk in my footsteps. They saw me and learned how to grow and be better. Before I knew it, they began to play ball as well, developing a keen interest in my coaching and being in most of the games. KJ had begun to play football in his high school. Keven also played football in his high school as well. The two of them went to different schools, of course, since my oldest lived in Columbia, Maryland with his mother. They were nine years apart in age but no matter what I still made sure I was there for both of them equally when they played their respective sports.

Coach Dr. Wilson and son Kevin Wilson Jr.

Time management was something I had a challenge with. It was difficult managing with everything going on but I tried to do my best. I ended up sacrificing the time I would normally set aside for myself, and spend it with my kids. Eventually, the management came automatically. It wasn't something I would think about. I learned that through my time in the military. There was a time when I had so many soldiers to handle at the same time. During that time, I had to manage my job, family, and everything else that I was responsible for.

I believe that what I learned during that time made it easier for me to manage it now. I had learned to prioritize the most important part of my day accordingly. I tried my best not to be unavailable for emergencies, or anything that my family would need me for. Military shaped too many aspects of my life and I began to learn that slowly as I progressed in life.

The first, I would say, above everything else was God. The second came my family, and then the third was the life I was building – my career. I kept my priorities in the same manner as well. I tried to coach my kids whenever I had the chance and they loved it. It was a family activity that we all looked forward to. When my kids reached high school, that was when they branched off on their own and I let them. I had to understand that they weren't kids anymore and had their own coaches at school who they preferred.

I didn't mind it, of course. They were reaching adulthood and had to begin making their own decisions. I guess them growing up gave me more leverage to begin more courses. I was now expanding my expertise and getting certified in different areas. I was becoming a basketball official and trying to learn all of the sides of the game. The problem was, and this was something not a lot of people understood, was that just because someone was a coach, it didn't mean they could play the game. I knew a lot of people who couldn't and yet were coaches. I wanted to be different – I had a passion for learning and growing and that's what I relied on. The certification helped me gain knowledge on both sides of the game. I learned the rules and regulations, how to perfect the game, and every angle of it. Eventually, I became the basketball and football official as well as a USATF and AAU track official.

Coach Dr. Kevin Wilson Sr. USATF Official

COACH DR. KEVIN WILSON SR

Coach Dr. Wilbon with his SMCA athlete track runner Jazmin Westbrooks

It was quite a journey and one that helped me grow beyond who I was. I never really counted them as part of my accomplishments because, I felt, it was always more like a hobby than a certification. The rest of my accomplishments were lined up though. I always wanted to grow my expertise in every area that caught my interest, and that's what I did. I gained certifications as a National Federation High School (NFHS) coach for basketball, football and baseball.

Once I had it all, I found out I was going to have another son. I was on top of the world once again. Chris and I named him Christian and whenever I looked at my sons together, I couldn't help but have my heart swell up with pride.

Coach Dr. Wilbon with his three sons; Kevin Jr, Kevon, and Christion

Kevin Jr., Kevon, and Christion are the reason for my immense happiness. Chris and I were complete and all of the kids worked hard doing their thing and trying to be the best versions of themselves. We couldn't be prouder of how our life turned out and were grateful for everything that life had to offer us. I sunk down in prayer and thanked God for all of His blessings. I knew my mom would be proud of me, and she would shower my kids with all the love she had in her heart.

I was thankful for every decision I had made throughout my life. I knew even the bad ones helped shape my life the way it was now. I would like the emphasis to be on that. There's no such thing as a bad decision. Every bad day has a reason behind it, a lesson that we don't see. It's only when time passes that we understand how much it impacted us and changed the trajectory of our life. That change might not always be welcome, but the reward for patience is always reaped later on in life. I've seen it happen more times than once. If nothing, I was able to learn the things that I shouldn't do, or the decisions that could be bad for me in the long run.

Coach Dr Wilson & Son Christian

When Christian came into our lives, we were all excited, including my sons. They all loved him and spent as much time as they could with him. Together, we were all able to help him through any problems he came across. The best part was that Christian had amazing big brothers to rely on. Whenever he felt he was in a fix that he couldn't talk to us about, he would turn to them. Both of them were ready to help him. I watched them grow into responsible men.

Kevon Wilbon Westlake HS Football Team

I knew that's what I wanted to do when I retired; I wanted to be with my son and watch him grow as well. I knew I didn't have to worry too much about my older sons. They walked their path, heading into universities and accomplish everything I couldn't accomplish at their age. Now, my attention would go to Christian. I couldn't believe how amazing he was and the kind of young man he was turning out to be. It was amazing. Kevin Jr. attended Virginia State University and graduated with his bachelor's degree, Kevon beat all of our expectations and got his associate degree at the College of Southern Maryland. Right after, he went to the University of Maryland, Global Campus in Maryland for his bachelor's degree from there.

Kevon Wilbon Graduating from University of Maryland Global Campus

Kevin Jr Virginia State University Graduate

11 time All-American, 4 Time Jr. Olympian Medalist track star with his 2021 , 1600M & 3200M All-American patches

Christian is really something else. He kept getting one accomplishment after another, exactly following my footsteps. Over the years, he only got better. He was inducted into the National Society for high school scholars with honors and maintained a GPA of 4.28 as a freshman in high school. This was an award that mostly 11 and 12th graders mainly achieved. He also ran track which earned him several gold medals. I have no doubt the kid is gifted.

Christian is an 11-time AAU All-American Track star and an 8-Time AAU Junior Olympian medalist with over 200 medals, 180 ribbons and 13 AAU Indoor national medals.

270 plus medals and ribbons with his All-American patches

He's even been in the Maryland Independent newspaper five times and received two Maryland Government Citations a Maryland Senate Citation and Maryland's 2018 AAU Track Most Outstanding Runner of the year for the 11-year-old boys.

Christian Wilson: Southern Sprinters

We took Christian to New York, New Jersey, Georgia and Virginia for track meets to get him better and run against top-quality runners in the country. Christian used his best qualities and put his own hard work in. He had a passion that we all saw and he turned that passion into greatness. Christian is an overachiever; he always was. He was able to take all of his activities in hand while also maintaining a high GPA, which says a lot about the kind of kid he is. The concept of balance is inexplicable. At such a young age, he was able to achieve more than what I had seen kids achieve, and he never boasted about it. One of Christian's best qualities was how humble he has always been and continued to be.

Coach Dr. Kevin Wilbon Sr. with his three boys, Christian, Kevon and Kevin Jr. In that order!

Chapter 12

"Success is not final; failure is not fatal: It is the courage to continue that counts."

Winston S. Churchill

My life has been an overview of struggle and through it all, I persevered for things I never expected. It's something I would love for my readers to understand as well – nothing is final. Struggle helps you to achieve greatness and through struggle we are all able to yearn for something more. Never let that yearning go to waste. It's only through this that we can all push ourselves and find a way out of our situation.

I started as a young boy with nothing but the will to survive, and I made my way to becoming a mentor, coach, author, military veteran, and educator. I'm also a USATF Official – which is the United States of America Track and Field official – and an AAU official, which stands for Amateur Athletic Union official.

Coach Dr. Kevin Wilson USATF Official working at a Indoor Track Meet

I'm also a National Federation High School (NFHS) basketball and track & field Official as well. I'm certified in almost everything that you can be certified in, and when it comes to sports, I'm certified at different levels in basketball, football, baseball, and track. So anytime I want to get out there and make some extra money, I can go do it with no problem. I officiate games and do everything that I can. At the same time, I'm helping my son because my son is one of the premier track runners in the country for a ninth-grader. Because I'm also the head track coach at my school, which gives me the right to talk to college coaches and scouts about my athletes in hopes of getting them scholarships. All through the years I relied on nothing but my motivation to change my destiny. I refused to end up with nothing, as I had seen all around me. I'm only sixty now, and in that short span of life, I learned and grew. I ensured that my life was fulfilling. I learned from everyone I came across in my path and I applied them on every step of my life – especially in my kids.

That's one of the things I loved about coaching as well – it's an art form. Coaching is precise and you need to be very careful when painting the masterpiece. To build champions, you have to adhere to the concept of perfection and aim for championship desires. You push to reach success and you don't have any take backs. The only way forward is to achieve the success you have in your mind. I wasn't taught, but I came up with the concept myself. I understood how, much like a painter, I had to paint my masterpiece through coaching. I had to pick the right colors, get the right picture in your mind, and work to ensure it becomes reality.

It's the concept I have about coaching, mentorship, and education. There are different cycles to it, but you have to build the right perspective and carry out the right steps. You don't stroke a brush and see what picture comes out of it – you get the picture in mind and then know how to stroke the brush, and what colors you're going to use.

Over the years, I established those steps for myself. I learned the order I had to have and then understand if I was missing any steps. It wasn't a chance that put me in the position I am today – I am everything because I followed the steps I made for myself. I also would like to praise God for the support I had. I knew that, at every step of the way, I had God by my side. Without him, I wouldn't have had the courage to achieve half the things I did.

Life is a series of learnings and you never stop. You grow from everything you see around you. I learned from my parents, my friends, strangers, kids, everyone. They each had a story to tell and had walked their own paths in life. I traveled to Germany, Korea, Saudi Arabia, and about 30 states in my military career and ran into a lot of people with wisdom. I absorbed it all and I would suggest that you, readers, do the same.

Progress stops when you believe you have achieved everything you're supposed to and nobody can teach you anything you don't know. Every story is a learning opportunity. Perhaps they went through something you couldn't even have fathomed, perhaps their courage is an inspiration to you. Perhaps I wrote something here that may be new to you. Much like you, I was eager to see my life too. I absorbed my surroundings like a sponge, absorbing everything and everyone I came across. Everything I am today is because of my ability to learn from those around me. I am able to achieve my path today mainly because I absorbed what I was taught, and from the people who surrounded me. So while I praise God every day for helping me, I also thank the people – good or bad – for teaching me something I couldn't otherwise learn. Just remember, nothing is all bad. Whether it's a situation or a person, it's always an opportunity to grow and that is good. While people do bad things, you can always see how they walk through it and come out of it. You can learn the things you can avoid and the consequences for your actions. For example, when I was in school and had begun to hang out with the wrong crowd, I became a different person. While I knew I was doing something wrong, it didn't dawn on me that I was on the wrong path. I saw the consequences my friend faced and how he wasn't going to change. I didn't want that for myself; I had a certain type of life I had to achieve. It created a change in me; the fear built a vision in me and a fear for my future.

That epiphany awoke my need for growth, and if it wasn't for that, I don't think I would have achieved half the things I achieved right now. It's all about perspective; I've seen people get shot, robbed, locked up, bullied, and go through so much more. It was never something I wanted to do. I never wanted to hurt anyone. It was never easy to face though and altered my path significantly from where I was originally headed.

My perspective changed – I didn't want to live a life like that. One of the main things was the number of funerals I attended. I witnessed so many of my friends die, it made me wonder what my own life was going to be like. Did I really want to walk the same path as they did? Did I want to keep struggling to make ends meet but only end up six feet under? What made me different from the people I had seen in my life? It was simple – I was adamant to creating my own opportunities instead of taking the easy way out.

When I had KI, it was the first time that I thought of anyone apart from myself. When I looked around me then, everything seemed brand new – my experiences were significant at that moment; I needed to build his. My kids had to have a life where they didn't have too much trouble on their hands. They had to grow to make a difference, and they did. I taught them the concept of hard work and we shared the same values. I told them, "You don't have to live by the way someone else wants you to live. If you want something out of life, you have to work for it. And if you want something out of life, it's going to be hard to get; nothing easy is worth having. Because if it's that easy, everybody would have it."

The thing is that if earning was easy and there were quicker ways to make money, then everyone would be doing it. Greatness is never easy – it's earned through hard work and perseverance. You have to go after it to ensure you receive it.

One of the things I've seen people do is procrastinate – they put things off for tomorrow. They believe that 'tomorrow' will hold more opportunities to get things done. However, the truth is that 'tomorrow' is never a guarantee. You cannot predict circumstances or the situations you're in. It's always a 'now-or-never' situation when you have to do something. Fix your mind on what you want to achieve and then go for it. Chances are, what you have your mind on will be gone in the blink of an eye. You cannot predict life – all you need is a plan and the ability to get things done at that moment. Once you gain the motivation for success and change your situation, there's nothing that will stop your plans.

Through every step of my life, I have learned that if there's something you want, you have to go after it and not wait for the right opportunity. There never is one. I had thought about this a lot and it often crossed my mind whenever I had an idea I wanted to work on even if it was the simplest thing. If I had listened to my inner laziness and waited for the right moment or opportunity to do something, I would have retired a long time ago with nothing to look forward to. My kids would not have reached their position today, and we would all be struggling for a decent life.

This is not a discouragement for you, but instead, the motivation that you need to do things the moment you get the idea. Make things work according to you so that, when it does, you hold no regrets when you're laying on your death bed looking back on your life. You can easily know that you fulfilled your purpose and didn't miss any opportunity.

Everything I'm doing now is what I want to do. I want to try to cement the foundation of my life and build a legacy for people to follow, especially my kids. I've always aimed for greatness, and now, I want everyone to see that, my kids' father was no ordinary man. They can easily say that I had a purpose in life and they should have a purpose in life too. It's easy to survive, but to actually live, you have to ensure that you push your boundaries and be seen.

I've seen a lot of people make this mistake – this mistake about existence and survival for living. All most of us do on earth is take up space and not work to ensure that we matter. We don't do half of the things that we should be doing. As I backtrack on my life, I see that I didn't just get five degrees and get inducted in seven prestigious honor societies, but I was also in a gospel group that's traveled around and witnessed to people young and old.

Coach Dr Wilson & Gospel Group The Committed Sons

Together, we witnessed how it felt to talk to seniors about God and how they felt about their lives. It was an eye-opening experience and yet another thing I could learn from. I saw how many people regretted the little things in life and wished they had made things better. It was these that I pointed to my kids, ensuring that my values were better instilled in them once they understood what I meant.

My kids and I would visit senior citizens when I retired from the military and became a mentor and coach. I began to go to church faithfully, sing in the choir, become a usher and basically do whatever my heart desired from me. I did it because I wanted to do something for everyone around me. That was the value my parents instilled in me. They had told me to always give back what was given to me and I followed that path. They taught me to be grateful for everything I had, regardless of the situation I was facing, and to praise God. I adhered to that as strictly as I could and made sure my family did too. My family and I are all about church. We believe in God, in the highest source, and in that nothing is possible without Him.

That's one of the reasons why I was able to achieve so much more with my life.

God helped me create my business Wilson Basketball Incorporation (WBI) and it was all done by myself. Then after years of coaching, instructing and mentoring through my business, I ran into my partner John. We later created a joint venture business we called it the ABC/WBI – Youth Conditioning and Fundamentals (YCF). This business is a fitness program where we let our clients come to us. We have kids from five years old to eighteen who we help create their diet plans, ensure that they eat right, and build their lifestyle right. But we don't just focus on the fitness and sporting aspect of it; we also mentor them on life in general.

We coach them on jobs, how to prepare for the next step, and how to create a life where they can succeed. On top of that, I still coach the track team at Southern Maryland Christian Academy, and I'm the head track coach for the middle school and high school athletes, boys and girls. I never let my age stop me from pushing myself. I've had people ask me how I'm still doing this at sixty years old and I tell them the same thing – it's all about motivation and perseverance.

Figure 1Coach Dr. Kevin Wilson Sr. and the Southern Maryland Christian Academy Track Team

I don't believe that age is a factor to consider when you want to achieve something. I maintained my lifestyle in such a way that I was able to remain fit even at this age. I never drank and I still don't drink, I eat right, exercise, never did drugs, never smoked, and made sure that I was always on top of the game. I never let peer pressure get to me. At the end of the day I made my own decisions.

Life is about choices, and the choices that you make will be the consequences you either enjoy or suffer later on in life. If you make good choices then you'll get rewarded. I'm willing to spread my knowledge to those who are willing to listen to me and live by what I tell them. I want to make myself as an example to people who wonder if they could achieve anything based on their circumstances. I've seen mentors who grew up with everything achieve the best and, at the end of the day, no one listens because they believe privilege comes into play. But I didn't have privilege throughout my life. I earned whatever I have now, and I make sure that I continue to set that as the basis for everyone trying to improve their lives.

It doesn't matter if you grew up in a bad neighborhood, you'll still be able to come out of it and do the things that you need to do, and I'm the example of that. I've set my kids as an example; I've ensured that people understand that there is success in living on the right path and putting in the hard work.

Life was difficult and there were moments where I wanted to give up – I am human, after all. There were moments when life was too tough for me to handle and I simply wanted to let everything go. But because I chose not to, I now enjoy life based on what I learned and experienced. I got the opportunity to travel the world and connect with so many people with so many stories. I conditioned the youth for any circumstances they may face.

When I look at these kids and then my own sons, I see the things that they miss. Most of the time its support, other times it's finances. In either of the case, it's important to know that there's nothing that cannot be overcome. If I can overcome it at a time when the world was still adapting to technical changes, then so can you.

Through me, my sons learned to push themselves. My youngest is a 4.28 GPA student who scored all A's in his report cards in high school. My three sons will reach the places they want to reach. I truly believe they will outdo me in everything and it's all because they put in the hard work to succeed. I believe that they can set an example just as I have. It's something that everyone can learn from – life is becoming more competitive by the day. You need to stay on your toes if you want to survive, and the way to do that is to put in effort with everything you do constantly. If you slack then you're going to lose on any opportunity that you get. It's not easy for anyone regardless of how many degrees you have, and the only way to stay on top of the game is to ensure that you're always one step ahead.

God has a plan for you, just like He has a plan for everyone else, but He gives to those who put in the effort to get. He will prioritize you if you prioritize Him and your success. You have to acknowledge the opportunities and recognize the ones you have to avail before it's too late. Most of the time, it's disguised with darkness and it would beat you down. However, if you allow it to destroy you, you may not get to where you have to. Life is tricky, but it's all about knowing your circumstances and proceeding accordingly.

I need to move forward according to my priorities, and I placed my priorities in a way to ensure that my God came first, then my family, and then anything else I needed. Eventually, everything would come down accordingly to plan.

I'd really want you – the person whose reading this – to know that there is nothing in the world that is unachievable. All you have to do is believe for every idea that comes to your mind. Through this belief, you would be able to put the time, effort, and your heart and soul into what you want. You can work on it while simultaneously taking care of the rest of your prioritised things.

But for every step you move in this world, vow to help others as well. You need to keep in mind that other people on your journey allow you to take that push. Similarly, there are always others on your journey who you can help as well. Looking back at my own path, I can't help but imagine where I would be if I hadn't met half the people I did. Because of them, I was able to reach where I did.

Just like them, I wasn't selfish when it came to imparting my knowledge and experiences, and you shouldn't be either. I could have been selfish and simply focused on my future. Instead, I made sure that everything I did was out in the open for others to learn from. I made sure my main purpose was clear – give back what I gained.

From that point on, I wanted to write this book; it further reiterates the point that I want to focus on. I want to give out my own knowledge to people on a broader scale. Through this book, I want to resonate to people and ensure that we all work together to better our communities. As a whole, I believe that I hold the passion most people do; the difference is that I worked on my passion and set aside the troubles that I faced growing up. When I look at the people around me, I notice that they are stuck in that phase and allow the depression of their past to overshadow the potential they hold. Every greatness is hidden between the cracks of your life. Your troubles are those cracks, and instead of allowing it to go deeper and rip your life apart, learn how to create the art

Structure your life to and think about the things waiting in your future. Always remember to envision your future in the best way possible, that's the motivation you need to put in the efforts. Find a way out of your circumstance by using everything at your disposal. Anything is possible.

I'm not saying that my life changed because of the military, and that's the only solution you might have too – what I'm saying is that you need to look for opportunities that could benefit you. I have seen so many people join the military and then retire. Similarly, I've also seen people who gained a degree then never pursued their careers. There's always an excuse that will keep you from moving ahead. It's up to you how you make the change. Most of the people I've seen retire after they have enough money saved up so they can grow old while watching their kids and grandkids grow up. However, I believe that your retirement shouldn't be the end of your career. Yes, you work so you can have a peaceful life, but what happens when all that money runs out? What happens when you do so much in your life but you look at the generations after you and notice that all of the efforts you put in for a change has all gone to vain?

Everything needs consistency, and these days, that consistency can be sought through continuous efforts. I want to place emphasis on always focusing on never giving up continually. I didn't give up after leaving the military, and I didn't give up after getting my doctorate. I continued to start over regardless of the difficulties I faced in my life.

As a kid, the situation is different; you can focus on building your career without added responsibilities. But after you gain the duties, it shouldn't be an obstacle in your journey to success. I had to do extra courses even after I had my kids. However, I knew that it was something I needed to do. I would say that military, regardless of how time-consuming it was, it still wasn't as challenging as what I faced after I retired.

The most difficult part was starting the dissertation. It was during the time when school was closing and I was going to lose all of the credits I had worked so hard to achieve. I needed to find a way and get myself out of the situation. Instead of simply focusing on the obstacles coming my way, I began to find a solution. The only one in mind was searching for another university that would accept my credits. The university I was in was closing down due to shady, financial troubles. At the time, I was in my third year and I had my family to worry about as well. The university took our money and there was no way to get the money back. At that time, I didn't just lose out on my time but also a lot of the money I had invested into this. When I joined another school, it was the most upsetting moment of my life because I lost everything I had worked so hard to achieve. Three years of struggle had gone down the drain and I was ready to give up. I talked to a lot of my family and friends, and they gave me the boost I needed when I was at my lowest. They told me, "Kevin, you haven't come so far in life just so you can quit. You've adopted the concept of pushing yourself; you've given your all in everything you do. You need to keep going."

Coach Dr. Wilson addressing the audience during a Motivational Speech

However, while I knew they were right, another part of me still questioned it. My mental health at that point had reached an all-time low. It was difficult to do – that time was rough and everything I thought about at the time, my mind convinced me was a bad idea.

"If you start and something like this repeats itself, you won't get very far. It's not worth it," I would keep thinking. However, the more I thought about it and indulged myself in other people's thoughts, the more I began to understand that, where you lack, there other others who don't. I had to allow myself to listen to what I was being told. I had to open myself to different ideas.

There were also a lot of my own ideas that other people didn't like. Many times, I felt like the world was against me because I would also come across people who pushed me down. Every struggle I mentioned with be refuted by,

"Well, you know, you've always had everything happen for you. Your life is easy."

They didn't realize, or refused to see, the struggles that I had faced and was still facing. The thing is, people quit and this hinders their progress. People who don't quit and reach success are automatically known to have it 'easy.' My lifestyle had gotten me that label. I, on the other hand, refused to let it happen.

I gained a newfound bout of courage, mainly by seeing my family and how they were living. I compared myself to who I used to be and I knew, in that moment, that I wasn't ready to let a simple backtrack bring down my entire belief system. I worked on my paperwork, put in the extra hours, and eventually, graduated with a 4.0 GPA.

How I did that? Well, it was a whole new journey in itself. When my university closed down, I began to look for other suitable options until I found North Central University. They made me take at least five courses before they accepted me. I was mad because they practically asked me to repeat everything. I realized later how it was for my own benefit.

I put in extra hours than I normally did, and after a lot of effort, I was able to achieve what I began so many years ago. I ended up doing a doctorate in education.

Quite frankly, it wasn't something I had initially planned. I had begun with something else in mind, but I had to begin anew when I joined North Central University. Their condition was that, for my minor, I had to do educational leadership.

I hadn't realized it when the trouble with my first university began, but North Central University was a blessing in disguise. The education was better, I scored better, and I also ended up being inducted into seven prestigious honor societies.

Once again, it's a point that I keep pushing towards with my readers; your troubles seem like the end when it happens. Yes, the mental effects of it last a very long time, and not everyone has the strength to push past it and move towards something better. However, the more you think about it, the worse it becomes. The way I wasted my time at my first university, I also learned from it. I learned the signs to look out for, and I kept everything I learned from my courses there.

It felt like the end for me when it was closing down, but if I hadn't pushed myself to move past that little obstacle, I wouldn't have achieved the score I did.

I look at my kids and see that they learned the same thing from me. Christian, especially, is the kid who safeguarded my struggles and learned from him. In the case of my older two sons, they achieved success just like me graduating from college obtaining their degrees and ultimately working and taking care of their business. My son Kevon is a visionary and a poet and knows his way around technology dealing with computers, music, sounds and videos. Kevin Jr. is a valiant blue-collar hard worker working for the city of Baltimore.

The thing with Kevin Jr. is I really wasn't around him as much as my other two sons because during that time, I was deployed mainly by the military but with Kevon and Christian, I was there for most of their entire lives being in the military stationed in the area then ultimately retired and mostly at home. I got to spend more time with them and teaching them the way I went about things and handled them. I had tried to give my sons most of my time and I had managed to do that. I coached them, taught them, and made sure they knew the impact of every decision.

All of my kids hold the same amount of love in my heart, I treasure them deeply and they truly are my sense of pride. They walk in my footsteps every day, proving to me that their growth is the most important success. Like me, each of my boys played football, basketball, and baseball. They excelled in each one.

Christian is the smartest kid I've seen but my other two sons are just as smart. Kevon is intelligent, and he worked the most he could and received two degrees a associates and a bachelors. He writes poems and is very articulate. KJ works as a house inspector in Baltimore and has a bachelor's degree in business. All of my boys focus on excelling in their lives and imparting their knowledge onto others.

There's no greater pride than that.

When it comes to my kids, I make sure that I'm there whenever they need me, but never smother them with my affection. I ensure that they are free to learn on their own. I have been questioned several times about Christian as well. He's not in the school where I coach and people often ask me why that is. It's odd for a lot of people because they always believe that kids should have help from their parents as much as possible. So if I coach in a school, my kids should study from the same school so I'm there watching them at all times.

The problem is that it doesn't build their confidence. Others also would start to believe that I'm favoring my kid when, in reality, that isn't true. I know my kids' capabilities and I ensure that he learns it on his own. I know my son is capable of handling himself and doesn't need me there every step of the way, so I sent him to a different school.

I want to reiterate the concept of hard work into my kids, and I have successfully done so. Everything my kids earned, they earned by themselves. They grew, learned, and became successful human beings all on their own. That doesn't mean I'm not there for them – I am. I am there whenever they want to talk, or if they want advice, or if they're stuck in a conundrum. I'm there because I'm their father and it's my job to ensure that they are never left on their own.

I look at Christian and I know that he has the ability to be better than I ever could be. He wakes up every day saying the same thing, "I did not wake up to be mediocre."

He believes in greatness – in his own greatness – and he's embedded it into his mind as well. At the same time, I lecture him all the time as well. I tell him to focus on school and education; I tell him how he can never achieve anything if he doesn't have an education. Yes, he's great at sports but sports can only take you so far. He's a track champion, but if he breaks his leg and can never play sports again, what's his backup plan?

Understanding the importance of what you can do and what you should do is significant. It's something that parents need to understand as well. Teach your kids the importance of believing in what they love. Teach them that they can do anything they put their minds to– see their passion as their success. But at the same time, also teach them to have a backup plan. Success is never achieved if you solely focus on one thing.

If you're good at sports, play sports, but take your education side by side. Take your humanity side by side as well. Never think you're better than everyone else because there's always going to be someone better than you. The difference should always be your attitude and your willingness to grow.

One of the things I've also taught my children is attitude. You can't always believe that you are better than the next person, and you can't run your mouth or trash talk people. You never have to prove anything to anyone else; all you have to do is make sure you live your life as a strategy. Understand the complexity of the human mind before you come out of your comfort zone and beat on someone else.

I let my own actions be an example to my kids. For starters, I allow myself to be known as Kevin Wilson Sr. I never let anyone call me a doctor because my title doesn't define me.

"Before all else, I'm a reasonable human being."

It's a quote that I try to teach my kids as well. Focus on building up your attitude and focus on knowing the right path to do things. The world today is laden with easy-way-outs. There's always a quick way to make money and please people. However, it's not always the way to make a living. Growing up, I saw people who chose the easier path out of their circumstances. They chose to live in the lane that led to their ultimate destruction. I saw how they sabotaged not just their lives but also their families.

I knew I didn't want that for myself or for my family. When I look at my kids, I'm afraid of the fact that they might do it too. But I know them, and I know how much they rely on struggling to reach the right goal. The shortcuts life presents have no meaning to them because they want to live the life that I was able to provide for them. I'm not saying that everyone I grew up with failed, some of the people I know ended up going to the MLB, NFL, or NBA. They achieved greatness through the hard work they put in. However, the difference between them and the rest of the people was not that they had a gift and others don't. It was the fact that they saw their passions and what they could do. Eventually, they managed by putting their mind in the right direction and achieving the best they could.

For me, everything I achieved was my passion – this book is my passion and my story. I teach so I can impart my passion and I can become better than I was. I want to create an environment where people are able to follow my footsteps and become decent beings as well.

Finally, I would like to ensure that those of you who have reached the end understand that there is greatness you have within you. You have the ability to be so much more than you believe. For every darkness that you have in your life, it's God's way of pushing you to do better. He's hiding a life of ease and security behind a little obstacle you meet in your path.

Don't give up on your dream, and always make sure that you put in a 100% in everything you do. At the end of the day, you let others define you the way you define yourself. For you, your family, and everyone who you may come across, be the best version you can be. Remember – struggle is success.

Head Coach Dr. Wilbon with 2022 SMCA High School & Middle School Boys & Girls Track Team

Head Coach Dr. Wilbon with his SMCA High School Girls 2002 MISAL Champions

Coach Dr. Kevin Wilson with his 5 Maryland State Championship rings in Varsity High School Basketball and Varsity High School Track and Field from 1998-2022